Guy Smith

The Cabinet of Curiosities

Book One

Michael Terence
Publishing

This edition first published in paperback by
Michael Terence Publishing in 2021
www.mtp.agency

ISBN 9781800942769

For Dad

Chapter One

It was the most boring place on earth.

Actually, that wasn't quite true. There had been that village at what seemed like the very edge of the civilised world - somewhere in wildest Wales - that had come close. Now that was definitely lacking in excitement. Except for the day that they had all decided to go *exploring* away from their camp site. When all three of them had climbed that barbed wire fence and ignored those 'Danger of Death' Ministry of Defence signs - now *that* had raised the tempo of their holiday quite a bit. Max had often wondered what kind of parents took their children on holiday to a village next to a military firing range - to be shot at *and everything*. Well, now he had his answer. They were the sort of parents who, not content with trying to have their children assassinated last summer, had now decided to bore them to death instead. Their grand plan seemed to consist of visiting this big, old house owned by the National Trust and it was here that Max was currently holding back a very big yawn - one of the early symptoms of the onset of death by boredom.

He looked around the room, fighting to keep his usually keen brown eyes open. From floor to very high ceiling, the walls were covered in dark, polished oak arranged in perfectly square panels. Some panels contained dark portraits of pale-skinned lords and ladies from hundreds of years ago. They all had very suspicious expressions- like they were wanted for ancient crimes. Other panels were just highly polished dark wood.

His mind drifted again to other dangerous visits. A vacational firing range hadn't been Max's only brush with death. Absolutely not. He remembered being taken on another holiday - to the East Coast one April. It was in Lincolnshire - he could see it now. Whilst walking the dog on a hurricane blasted beach, with waves that would have been comfortably at home in any tsunami (not to mention the genuine Easter blizzard that complemented the

1

raging sea) they had returned to their caravan to discover that it had been blown clean over a sea wall and was floating upside down in the nearby boating lake. Imagine if they hadn't gone walking the dog that morning. They too would have been floating upside down in that boating lake. The more he thought about it, the more it seemed that his parents didn't actually like their children and were determined to get rid of them through an assorted mix of planned and, perhaps even, expected natural disasters.

Max struggled to focus again. Currently, Mr and Mrs Foster - those clearly dangerous parents - were nodding in fascination whilst listening to the Tour Guide who was caressing the wood panelling a little too lovingly. Mum and Dad liked to think they were 'cool'. Dad had just bought himself the most ridiculous pair of thick-framed glasses which he insisted were 'trendy' - even the word he chose to describe them had passed into ancient history. Max hadn't believed anything could be more embarrassing than those mustard coloured corduroy trousers and that flowery shirt but the spectacles were worse. All they achieved was to hold back the two sides of his centrally parted fringe from closing like curtains over his eyebrows. Mum was just as embarrasing. She had recently taken up knitting to 'save money on the latest fashions'. How Mum was going to make the latest fashions using 1950's knitting patterns, Max wasn't sure but he was absolutely not going to wear those itchy, three-quarter length shorts!

The Tour Guide wouldn't have looked out of place in them though. She seemed to favour a ghastly mix of slightly differing shades of brown - the sort that managed to make your clothes look like they always needed a good wash. Her tour was just as dull as her favourite browns. Max tried hard to concentrate again - actually focusing on her speech for a moment. Apparently - "Internal oak wall panelling had been an important part of the English aristocratic family home for over four centuries," the brown Tour Guide was droning on and Max stifled another yawn.

This needed far too much concentration for a Saturday morning. Didn't she understand he was only 'very nearly twelve'?

Didn't she understand that he wanted to watch TV, or play on his console or take his bike out? He would *even* consider taking his bike out *in the rain* to escape this. He may even agree to put a comb through his unkempt mop of blonde hair; things were getting that desperate.

"Kensington Castle was constructed as the country residence of Sir Walter Cope in 1582," the woman in brown continued.

It was clear to Max that she just didn't understand the needs of some of her audience.

Max looked back at his two sisters. Surely they must have been as fed up as he was. It was mildly re-assuring to discover that they were. Kira, his big sister, had her head lowered - long auburn hair cascading forward over her denim jacket. She was messaging again. Her fingers had been permanently attached to the screen of her new phone ever since she'd got it as a fourteenth birthday present. Now, she was ever so grown up. Even though she was in touch with the exciting outside world of her friends, her face was fixed in a blank expression as she glanced up at Max - confirmation of the early stages of a case of death by boredom indeed. Chloe, his little sister, scuffed her right foot repeatedly across the polished wooden floor, her little white trainers making a faint squeak as they touched. Her glazed expression as she stared into space was just as telling - onset of boredom well and truly established. After all, what normal six-year-old would want to listen to the finer details of 16th century interior decorating - not the sort of information you would get from kids TV. She blew air upwards from her bottom lip and her fringe raised in sync with her disbelieving eyebrows. Shaking herself conscious again, her two dark blonde pigtails bounced with an enthusiasm that was lacking everywhere else in the room.

Suddenly, Max had that shoulder-raising feeling that he was being watched - in fact, all three of the Foster siblings were being very closely observed. In an instant, and through years of finely tuned practice, the childrens' expressions changed. Kira's mobile was removed from sight as her hand was quickly hidden behind her back - the phone slipped smoothly into her jeans and, in perfect synchronicity, her other hand rose and swiftly slid her glasses on to her nose. These were the glasses she wore when she was trying to look intelligent. Her clever specs. Although, to be fair to Kira, she really was intelligent - Max would, of course, never admit this in public. (Not even under torture would he make that announcement.) Chloe had stopped that repetitive scuffing and was now twisting one of her hair bunches with her left hand; her head was tilted at that annoying angle she used when she wanted to look like a cute six-year-old. Both his sisters were smiling intensely - almost painfully with the over exertion of fake enthusiasm.

Big fake smiles could only mean one thing - the parents were looking! Quick as a flash, Max whirled round, his expression swiftly changing to one that he thought would show his keen intelligence. He found himself nodding and striking a pose with his hand supporting his chin - thumb and finger in a v-shape either side of his face. Clearly that would show great interest in this exciting world of oak. He hoped his parents wouldn't be testing him on what he'd learned during the car journey home - but he wouldn't put it past them.

Wait - the parents were smiling too. Smiling and waving with proud expressions for their three, clearly fascinated, offspring. The parents had bought it. They actually believed that he and his sisters were in a state of intellectual enjoyment. The parents turned back to face the brown tour lady and, in relieved unison with his sisters, Max dropped his fake expression. After all, maintaining that much enthusiasm could actually be harmful. Everyone knew that. It was also a well known fact that 'very nearly twelve'-year-old boys could only concentrate for a maximum period of thirty seconds; unless of course, football or food or fighting was involved. Or, better still, all three.

Still, the Tour Guide continued, "If you would like to follow me, ladies and gentlemen, we will now go and look at a wonderful, curving, oak Tudor staircase. Look out for the carved animal heads; one of which represents a tale from Aesop!"

This was too much. Max turned back to his sisters. He saw

that the smartphone and the trainer scuffing had returned. Both Kira and Chloe looked at him with desperate, pleading expressions.

"Wonderful, curving, Tudor staircase?" he asked sarcastically.

"Errr - No!" spat Kira through gritted teeth.

"Fascinating example of oak panelling?" Max continued.

"No, thanks!" added Chloe with equal disgust.

Max had spotted something, "Closed door, marked 'No Entry'?"

"Now you're talking!" Kira sounded keen.

"Let's!" squeaked Chloe, excitedly.

And so, as the tour party continued on its oak-panelled odyssey, Max placed his hand on a heavy, Tudor door latch. And, as his Mum and Dad left with the other tourists, the three children stayed behind.

Max hesitantly lifted that Tudor door latch.

The door wasn't locked.

Chapter Two

With the heavy metal clunk of a very old and equally reluctant latch, the door groaned slowly open as if not keen to reveal what it was hiding. The three of them stood in the wide frame peering into a dusty uncertainty. The wait seemed difficult to judge - almost timeless.

"Oh, littlest first!" Chloe broke the awe and strode impatiently through the opening seeming to disappear. "Woah!" came her expression from somewhere beyond.

Max exchanged hurried glances of reassurance with Kira and, together, they stepped across the threshold.

A high leaded window cast broken, dusty sunlight on the most incredible room Max had ever seen. Shelves, alcoves, cubby-holes, boxes, chests, crates and tables were everywhere along the panelled walls - panels that were, of course, all made of the same dark oak. Every possible means of storage within that room was filled to capacity with a dazzling array of different objects.

"Cool," he whispered.

"What on earth?" asked Kira.

"Woah!" repeated Chloe. A girl of few words but many expressive sounds.

On closer inspection, Max could see that all the items in the room were actually labelled. A small faded, cream-coloured tag was attached to every single thing. This was no small achievement as there were hundreds of bits and pieces and each seemed to be catalogued in the same neat, italic handwriting. The room itself wasn't big but it was full to bursting point with this collection - a collection that had obviously come from all over the world.

"A back-scratcher from India, 1603," Max read the label of a gruesome-looking elongated fork with a handle covered in what he thought must be monkey fur.

"Inuit Eskimo Orca carving from the Northern Territories, 1811," Kira was studying a stylised little ivory statue of a killer whale. She had a thing about whales and dolphins.

"A chain made of monkey teeth, Ma-lay-si-a," Chloe struggled with the name of the country. "Monkey teeth? Yuk!" She dropped the necklace back into its ornate box.

This was a collection that had obviously been gathered over a great deal of time. Painstakingly assembled in this dusty room and, rather sadly hidden from the general public on their historic tour by a 'No Entry' sign. Max had a nagging thought - the atmosphere of the room clearly showed the passage of time, with dust sparkling and dancing in the filtered sunbeams that penetrated from outside, but the objects looked fresh. Almost as if recently made and newly collected.

"The horn of a bull seal," Chloe was inquisitively rummaging as Max dismissed his thoughts as a trick of the light. "What's a bull seal?"

"A male seal," answered Kira, more interested in the rather beautiful little killer whale.

"Seals don't have horns," Chloe continued angrily, "Even I know that!"

"Maybe it was a Walrus then," Max said distractedly, his attention suddenly drawn elsewhere again. "Now, this is interesting," he paused, "The dagger that killed Julius Caesar in 44 B.C." He held it up and his imagination was momentarily captured by the glint of sunlight reflected from a shiny and very keen knife-edge. Max wondered where this blade had been; what it had been involved in; who had held this handle? History suddenly seemed very real indeed. His mind was quickly full of vivid past times. Past times that he could almost touch - almost be part of. He shook his head suddenly, breaking an epic chain of thought and dropping back into the calmer here and now. "As if!" he exclaimed re-assuring himself, though deep down a little confused by the rush of ecxitement he had suddenly felt.

"Doubt it," said a rather muffled Kira who was now behind a pile of stuff labelled as 'The Holy Relics from a Spanish Galleon, 1580'.

"Julia, who?" asked Chloe.

"Julius Caesar. Famous Roman. Murdered," added Kira knowledgeably but disinterestedly half-pointing in the direction of her brother, "With that, apparently."

Max held on to the dagger, almost with a subconscious urge not to let go, whilst continuing to read more labels around him. This really was much more interesting than the rest of the stuffy house. For once, his total concentration had been caught; here and now in this timeless historical room. If only his parents could see him now - actually paying attention and everything. "Henry Irving's sandal, 1892. The baubles of Henry VIII's fool, 1512." Then a disappointed realisation started to set in. "Oh, come on," he groaned, "Shakespeare's quill, 1599. Yeah, right."

Chloe crossed to Max and they both looked down at a seemingly freshly-plucked feather in one of his hands, still apparently wet with the ink of 1599, and the dagger in his other, glinting impossibly after a couple of thousand years. Both items were, however, very confidently labelled. "What is this place?" she asked him.

"Some sort of collection. A collection of old things, like…" Max was cut short.

"Like a museum. Just like a museum!" said Kira more excitedly.

Max stared at her in disbelief. Only Kira could get that excited about a museum. All three now focused their attention as they stood around the large and heavily built central table. Neither Max nor his sisters had noticed the dust in the air ripple slightly as someone else had quietly entered the room.

"A Cabinet of Curiosities," came an announcement from

behind them.

They wheeled around together to see an impossibly old man. He was wearing a long, black coat embroidered with detailed oriental pictures - it could easily have formed part of the collection in the room and, indeed, Max found himself looking for his information label. The old man had long, white and very wispy hair with an equally long, white and very wispy beard. Odd as he looked, the impossibly old man was smiling kindly at them.

"Dumbledore!" thought Max, aloud.

"Santa!" gasped Chloe.

"Who... Where did you... What?" stammered Kira in an uncharacteristically non-intelligent kind of way.

"A Cabinet of Curiosities," repeated the impossibly old man.

Max had to ask, "What?" Then remembering his manners in front of strangers, "I'm sorry. I mean, Pardon?"

"Not a museum, my dears, but a Cabinet of Curiosities. *The* Cabinet of Curiosities, in fact. The *original*, you might say," his smiling face suddenly turned to concern and he continued, "I am sorry. I didn't mean to startle you."

"Who are you?" asked Chloe - with the very question that Max had been thinking but dare not ask.

"Oh, how terribly rude of me. I am Sir Walter Cope, Knight of Queen Elizabeth's College of Antiquaries and the owner of Kensington Castle." What could be seen of the smile, below all that beard, had returned and the old man's eyes positively sparkled with an infectious enthusiasm - he seemed keen to meet these curious youngsters.

Max was genuinely impressed. "A Knight? Cool!"

"He means that he's a 'sir'. It's only a title," cut in Kira.

Max was undeterred, she was not spoiling his thoughts, "He said he owns a castle."

The old man laughed. "Indeed I do, young sir. This is it," he gestured widely and slowly around him to suggest a big space. "The house in which you stand... Or should I say the room in which you... trespass? I really do not recall this particular room being part of the guided tour."

There was a long silence.

"We are... explorers," announced Chloe, hurriedly. Kira buried her face in her hands and shook her head with the sort of embarrassment specially reserved for younger sisters and brothers.

"Are you indeed? Then you have discovered my collection. Well done!" the old man beamed.

"Your Cabinet of Curiosities?" asked Kira.

"That's right, young lady. Within this very room is the celebrated collection of Sir Walter Cope. Started long ago in... ah, let me see, when was it? 1591 is the date I seem to recall. Though of course some of the exhibits are from much earlier times - and I do get increasingly confused as time goes by," the old man's face was suddenly very serious.

"It's old then," stated Chloe with conviction.

"Ancient," he nodded. "And very extensive. There are items here from the very four corners of the world."

"The world's round. It doesn't have corners," Chloe was determined that this stranger wasn't going to get away with any nonsense.

"Hmmm? Ah, of course, science has moved on so much since those early days of collecting. So many discoveries over the centuries..."

"It's fake, of course?" said Kira, as if annoyed that her time was being wasted. "The items are clearly fakes - forgeries. I mean Shakespeare's quill looks new and the dagger that killed Julius Caesar is far too shiny? Come on, they can't be original."

The old man seemed a little hurt by her remarks, "All were

painstakingly collected. Many in person."

"Well," said Chloe, "I think it's great. The Cupboard; I think it's fantastic!"

"Cabinet," corrected Kira in her official role of 'Patronising Elder Sibling in Charge'.

"Whatever."

The old man was looking about him with real pride, "Yes, it is, as you say, fantastic. I'm very glad that you appreciate it. You must all take a long look. Explore the items!" This was the cue that they had been waiting for and all three of them happily continued reading labels and examining objects. "But, wait. You young things must have parents. They will be worried about you."

Max shook his head and so did his sisters. Kira offered a further explanation. "You see, Mr. Cope, our parents will be so engrossed with carved, Tudor staircases they won't actually notice that we are missing."

The old man puzzled over this for a while then softened. "Well, the tour does end up outside in the corridor. You *shall* marvel at centuries of collected antiquaries until you hear your parents finish the tour outside. Be my guest. Enjoy the treasures, children. You may learn much from history you know." There were now three expressions of thanks and the old man was about to shuffle off when he seemed to remember something important. Something very important. His expression darkened and his eyes lost their sparkle, "Just one warning..." That got everyone's attention so he continued, "Many of these items come from dangerous times and hazardous places. Just remember this advice - from this very point here, take nothing but your memories and leave nothing but your footprints on this dusty floor. You see, time... well, it can be rather... complicated."

Max looked at his two sisters and he had a moment of thought, pondering dangerous times and hazardous places; and in that moment of thought, Sir Walter Cope had gone. As mysteriously as he had arrived, he had quite simply disappeared -

leaving nothing but a slight vibration in the sparkling sunlight dust.

"Take nothing but memories," echoed Kira.

"Leave nothing but footprints," continued Chloe.

"Very deep!" laughed Max snapping out of his thoughts with a bit too little respect. He turned to apologise to the old man for being too dismissive but saw that he was gone. "Forget Shakespeare's quill," he dropped the feather back on to the table, "Disappearing ancient bloke - now that is bizarre. Maybe he was a wizard. He had the beard!" His sisters didn't answer him, instead, they looked back at the place where Sir Walter had been. Max turned his attention back to the items and realised that, curiously, he was still holding the dagger. "This stuff is great though," he announced. "Look at it all. So much better than fusty old books! This is *hands on* history."

Kira was puzzled - as the oldest of the three; she often thought it was her task to worry a bit - like the adults did; she was, after all, the closest to being one of those adults. "Wonder what he meant though. Memories and footprints? Complicated time?" Max certainly wasn't listening. Instead, he had invented an amusing competition to see how many items of historical clothing he and Chloe could weigh themselves down with in one go. They had removed their own top layer, dumped it on the central table and pulled costume after costume from the dado rail of one of the walls. The result of trying them on made them look like very multicultural film extras.

It was Kira that noticed it first. "There's more!" she called in amazement. Max and Chloe looked at her with disgust. Of course there was more, Max thought, the whole room was crammed with the most amazing things. He carried on rummaging. The clothing had gotten too heavy so it was now strewn around the room. "Look," Kira went on with some urgency, "There are more rooms." Max and Chloe stopped. "Three more doors. Look. *Three more doors!*" She was right - there were three more oak panelled doors.

Max wielded his Roman dagger triumphantly and pointed at the middle door. "Bet there's loads more cool stuff!" He held out his other hand to grasp the door handle.

"Wait!" shouted Kira in her most adult voice, "Which one?" Chloe crossed to Kira's side and smiled at her, sensing she was cross.

Max lowered his arm and fiddled with the dagger. Reluctantly he gritted his teeth. "You choose, Kira," he muttered with some reluctance.

Kira looked at the doors. Studying them in turn whilst Max sighed in frustration. It was no good; there were no obvious differences; they were all the same. At last, Kira crossed to the furthest door and indicated that her brother and sister should join her. Then she placed her hand on the handle. "It's warm!" she cried and let go of the door, a little concerned.

"Oh, let me!" huffed Max and he grabbed the handle. It was warm. A strange but not unpleasant current was pulsing gently up his arm in a tickling wave - almost urging on what was to follow. He gripped the door handle tighter and held the dagger in his other hand with more urgency, like it was suddenly very important indeed.

Then it happened. Everything seemed to fall apart and collapse in on itself. The oak panels seemed to burst open and bright white light burned through their age old cracks. There was a grinding, wrenching sound as though someone was trying to rip the very room in two. Max wanted to shout out to his sisters but there wasn't time. Before he could scream anything at all, it was over.

Chapter Three

There was still a lot of very bright light but at least the movement had stopped and the horrible tearing noise had gone. It really was *very* bright though - very bright and, suddenly, much warmer. Max squinted as he opened an eye. There was brightness and blueness and there was nothing else. There was no land, no buildings and no scenery at all. There was just blueness with a few flecks of whiteness. He felt as if he must have been tumble dried. Max opened both eyes and started to panic. Where was the ground?

"Get up, Max," It was Kira's voice. If she wanted him to get up then he must be lying down. Of course, he knew that. He sat up quickly and what he saw made him want to lie straight back down again and close his eyes once more.

The brightness turned out to be the sun - that explained the warmth he could feel on his skin. The light seemed to be bouncing off of the great, big, buildings he appeared to be sitting in front of - great, big, *marble* buildings. Kira and Chloe were staring down at him. Chloe had her hands on her hips and was clearly not very impressed. She was holding back tears.

"Ah… hi," Max struggled for a sentence and failed miserably.

"Ah… look!" said Chloe, sharply.

Max looked further. There were pillars, imposing steps, statues and fountains. It seemed that they had exchanged dark oak for white marble. "Which room is this?" he asked pathetically, "The bathroom?"

"No. It's not," snapped Kira, "Try Rome."

"Rome?"

"Yes, Max, Rome and I think *Ancient* Rome at that."

Max laughed but got no smiles from his sisters. There was a pause. "You're serious, aren't you?" There was no reply. Max looked away from his sisters and took a closer look at this new place. With the warmth came a distantly familiar smell, the sort of smell you associate with holidays in the sun and a different kind of food - more exotic, he thought. Like their only family holiday abroad a couple of years ago in… the Mediterranean. There were people here too. People who seemed to be wearing sheets and even some men wearing what looked like short dresses. Next to him, two men in white and purple sheets were talking. Max listened in to their conversation for a moment.

"When did Rome ever have storms like the last few nights, Flavus? The gods are angry at something," said the dark-haired, taller one.

"Never, Marullus. The last time I stood in such a torrential downpour, I was on Caesar's ill-fated Briton campaign. 'Come to Britannia for the winter', he said - nothing but blue painted savages and awful weather!" replied the shorter bald man.

"He was just a general then though. Now he wants to be king of the known world…"

Max lost concentration. Rome? Caesar? He had thought floor to ceiling oak panelling was too much but this really was making his head hurt - and his leg was hurting too. He looked down to see if he was sat on something. He was. It was that dagger. The dagger that killed Julius Caesar. The dagger he had picked up from that impossible room and for some strange reason had not wanted to let go of.

"Get up, Max!" Kira was more insistent this time.

"What's going on? We can't be in Rome?"

"Great," said Kira, "Now he gets culture shock. Or maybe it's time lag!"

Max struggled to his feet, his mind racing. Kira was holding Chloe's hand and all three of them were silent. The moment was broken by the growing roar of a crowd - lively and coming their way.

15

"Come on! Over here!" Kira ran across the open square towards an up-ended cart, its straw covered load spilling on to the floor. They all gathered behind it, crouched and anxious.

Max's heart was pounding. "Could someone please get me up to speed? What's going on, Kira?" He got no reply though as a raucous mob burst into the square at the side of one of the pillared buildings. It was difficult to tell whether they were celebrating or rioting. The children looked on from behind the cart.

The two Romans in white and purple seemed to be trying to stop the mob. The one called Marullus was asking them what it was that they were celebrating and his reply was a one word chant - "Lupercalia!" The chant got louder and more threatening.

"What's the Lupercalia?" asked Max.

"A festival, young man," came the answer from a stranger. Max whirled round in alarm. "Don't be alarmed," the smiling man continued, "I think you're quite right to hide behind my cart."

"Your cart. Sorry, Mr... errr?"

"Sabre. Gaius Marcus Sabre, trader of ceramic goods. Not in need of a good set of amphora are you?"

"Am for who?"

"Amphora, Max. Vases for wine," Kira explained.

"Ah, no thank you, Mr. Sabre," Max stammered.

"You could tell us what's going on though," suggested Kira.

"Ah, you mean that lot," he pointed to the lively mob confronting the two important looking Romans and folded his arms across his bulky chest, "Well, today *is* the 15th day of February," The children stared back vacantly, not understanding the significance of the date. "The Feast of the Lupercal?" Gaius continued to enlighten confused expressions. "Mark Antony leads the Priests of the Julian College on a run through the streets of

Rome to celebrate the festival. It's great fun. Brings in huge crowds. I'll sell loads of amphora for the free wine," Gaius indicated his loaded cart then sank both his big hands into the front pocket of his battered leather apron to rattle a few loose coins. "They'll be gathering over there in the Forum to see the runners finish," he removed a hand from the pocket and pointed a tanned finger across the square, "And to see Caesar, of course."

"Julius Caesar?" asked Max.

"Of course. Where have you lot been lately? He's a hero. Some say he'll be the new King of Rome." Gaius' expression was distant, as if his big dark eyes had spotted something worrying in the distance.

Breaking Gaius' thoughts, the mob erupted in deafening chants of "Caesar! Caesar! Caeasar!" The children turned in time to see the celebrating crowd storm from the market place, clearly in search of Caesar. An eerie silence descended and the two more important Romans made their way past the cart in subversive conversation.

"Will you go and see Caesar?" asked Flavus.

"Not whilst I have a breath in my body," answered Marullus - and then the two important Romans were gone. Gaius had started to pack his amphora into the straw, picking stray bits of it from his tangled mop of brown hair. It seemed he was anticipating bigger sales if he followed the crowds.

Chloe broke the strained silence, "I don't understand."

"Me neither," agreed Kira.

"It's like *Gladiator*," thought Max aloud, "But more…"

"More real?" Kira stopped his imagination dead.

Chloe was getting tearful. Her big brown eyes welled as she looked up at Kira for guidance, "It can't be real, Kira. We just walked through a door."

"It's not real. Is it, Kira?" now Max needed re-assurance too.

"Well, if this is an exhibit in Kensington Castle, it makes the York Viking Museum look a bit lame." Kira really did seem as confused as her siblings.

Chloe was crying, "We just walked through a door."

"We did," said Max, "Where is it? Where's the door?"

"And Mum and Dad, Kira? Where are Mum and Dad?" Chloe pleaded.

"I don't know, Chloe. I don't know where they are," said Kira.

Max needed an explanation. It was all very well this kind of thing happening in stories; in science fiction or fantasy - that was acceptable; you could stop reading those tales; you could turn those films off or leave the room or change the channel if things got a bit unnerving. He closed his eyes and his mind whirled with impossible and unlikely explanations. He pinched himself hard and willed himself to wake up from this weird dream - but when he opened his eyes again, everything was just the same - the bright sun; the white marble; a muscular Roman market seller packing his strange vases onto his cart; and his two sisters, wide-eyed and totally confused. "We walked into the Cabinet room thing. We spoke to *Dumbledore*. We walked through another door and…"

"Into history, Max," said Kira, "We walked into history. Well, you wanted *hands on* history!"

Max was frantic now and yelling. Gaius stopped loading his cart and looked worriedly at this distressed little boy but Max wasn't looking back - he was confused and angry and he felt sick to the pit of his stomach. "This isn't history, Kira! It can't be. It's a trick! An illusion! A film set or something!" Max knew his ideas were desperate and his hope of a logical explanation evaporated.

Kira finished his hope off completely, "Look around you, Max. No cameras, no film crew, no trailers and very real marble."

"All right!" snapped Max, throwing the dagger to the floor and watching it slide across the flag stones. He looked up and skipped a breath as he saw Chloe sobbing quietly. He suddenly felt very selfish and very sorry, "It's all right, Chloe. Everything is going to be fine. We'll find that door and we'll go through it and everything will be like it was. You'll see."

Chloe was still sobbing but Kira hadn't seemed to notice. She was staring intently at the dagger lying a few metres away.

"Kira," Max started but she wasn't paying attention to him.

"You brought that with you, Max? That dagger?" she said.

"Yes, but Chloe…"

"You brought that dagger? To Ancient Rome?"

"Yes, but…" he wasn't following her chain of thought at all. She clearly was having one of her 'off on a tangent' moments.

"Or maybe it is why we are here. An ancient Roman dagger back in Ancient Rome."

This was a really big tangent.

"What are you talking about, Kira?" Max found himself walking back and picking up the dagger again, almost absent mindedly.

"Oh, nothing. Just a theory developing," Kira broke off and turned her attention from the dagger in Max's hand to her upset little sister, "Ok. Whatever is happening to us, we can sort it. Right?" There was no response from Chloe. "Right? I mean, we've had adventures before. Remember that Ministry of Defence firing range? We got out of that didn't we?"

"Teddy didn't." Chloe was still quite traumatised at the loss of Teddy. She had cried for two weeks and refused to go to bed, "They shot Teddy."

"Ok," struggled Kira, "But apart from Teddy…" Chloe was looking at Kira with real anger over the loss of her favourite cuddly toy and Max genuinely felt pity for her. Kira was knocked back by the intense emotion in Chloe's face and her morale boosting speech fell flat.

Max thought it best to step in and do his bit, "Yes, we did get out of there safely," Chloe's eyes welled with tears again, "And, we... we all remember Teddy with great fondness for the brave little bear that he was." There was a long silence between the three siblings. Max wondered if his appreciation of Teddy's finer qualities was enough.

"Ok. So what do we do?" Chloe had accepted his tribute to her lost bear and Max smiled reassuringly in response. In all honesty, he hadn't the faintest idea what to do.

Kira clearly had though, "We're looking for a door. The same door we left the Cabinet of Curiosities through. A Tudor, oak panelled door - marked 'No Entry'. In Ancient Rome." Now there was a paradox if ever there was one, thought Max as he tried to follow Kira's chain of thought. He didn't puzzle for long though as loud and very excited shouting brought his attention back to the Roman market place.

"What now?" asked Chloe.

"Well, ever heard the phrase 'When in Rome'?" Kira was getting blank looks, "Do as the Romans do? No? Never mind, let's go and see what they are shouting about." With that she strode off in the direction of the shouting. Max hated it when she did that - when she was just too confident.

"And don't forget that dagger, Max. I've a feeling it is important." Kira was now twenty metres ahead and calling back over her shoulder. Max thought she looked quite at home in Ancient Rome. Not that this was ancient to the Romans around him; to them, this moment was here and now - as modern as could be. He looked down at little Chloe and smiled. She smiled back and that could mean only one thing. They should follow their older sister.

Chapter Four

The square was full of *Ancient Romans*! It was like a historical version of one of those music festivals that their parents had gone on about enjoying so much when they were younger. Max recalled being a little disturbed when shown the photos of hundreds of people climbing barriers, speakers, portaloos and each other to get a view of a very distant and very minor celebrity somewhere in the driving rain. Dad would go all starry-eyed and stare into his care-free past recalling when he had flowing golden locks and mum had short auburn spikes and they had camped in muddy fields, listened to bands no-one had really heard of and gone without washing for days on end. This wondrous time was referred to as '*The* noughties'. He could just hear his Dad saying it - a big pause for effect then a deep and gravelly voice, like he was advertising a film at the cinema - '*The* noughties'. Mention of this time was usually followed with his smile fading and the statement, "Then the children came along and put a stop to all that."

Parents! Weren't they weird?

Mind you, Max would have given anything to hear his Dad say it right now. He would even have considered giving him a hug - if he could only spot him in the crowd. That would, of course, be the crowd of *Ancient Romans* in front of him. The reality check had failed again.

Kira had lead them through winding back alleys, chasing the sound of the cheering. Finally, they had rounded a corner and a packed square had opened up in front of them full of people jostling and clamouring, shouting and shrieking. There were eager children on their parent's shoulders, enthusiastic men and women hanging from over-looking windows and balconies, idle tradesmen standing attentively on their carts and stalls and even what appeared to be a group of very animated Roman soldiers demonstrating on a nearby roof. All eyes were fixed in one direction and the noise was deafening. All Ancient Roman life was here.

"This is the Forum," announced Kira as if she were a time-travelling tour operator. Max and Chloe stared back, blankly. "The main square for important events," she clarified.

"I can't see," moaned Chloe, "Who are they all looking at?"

Chloe got her answer from the crowd - all of them, in unison, like a football chant - "Caesar! Caesar! Caesar!" Max stretched to his full height which, as he was small for his age, wasn't very high. He could just make out a raised area at the top of some steps with a gathering of what must have been a better class of Roman. They were all finely dressed. The women wore lavish jewellery - earrings, necklaces and broaches - on their fine white and gold-edged dresses. The men wore more elaborate sheets edged with purple and gold. The group were complemented by armed soldiers standing menacingly between the grand pillars at the top of the imposing steps.

"Max, I can't see!" It was Chloe again.

"Let's try and get closer. Squeeze through the gaps. See what's going on," suggested Kira.

"I'll end up stabbing someone!" Max pointed to the dagger.

"Put it up your hoodie then," Kira was getting impatient to discover the source of all the commotion.

"I left it in the curiosities room!"

"Well, put it up your T-shirt then," Kira was really more concerned with the chaotic events in front of them.

"I'll end up stabbing *myself*!"

Before Max could conceal the dagger, a huge cheer rang out and the crowd span on their heels to face the opposite direction. For a moment, Max became very self-conscious wondering if they were looking at him. He quickly hid the dagger beneath his over large t-shirt and winced as it poked his chest. "Ouch! See!" he hissed, but his sisters weren't listening. They too had turned to look the other way and, on doing the same, Max couldn't believe his eyes - again.

Lots more people had gathered behind them but were now parting to make way for one of the strangest sights his young mind had been forced to comprehend. A line of athletic looking men wearing what appeared to be nappies made of animal skins were running towards them. More bizarrely still, they were carrying leather whips and were flicking people in the crowd who were too slow to get out of their way. Now this lot would have looked right at home at one of their parents' music festivals. Max moved and Kira dragged Chloe in the opposite direction so that they were facing him. The runners came closer.

"Hey!" yelped Kira clutching her arm. She obviously hadn't moved far enough.

"Oh, that was lucky, dear," said a smiling young Roman woman now at Kira's side.

"Lucky?"

"Oh, yes, dear," she went on, "What I wouldn't give to be flicked by the goatskin whip of a Priest of the Julii?" She touched Kira's cheek affectionately. "You'll be having many strong sons, that's for sure."

Kira was actually speechless. Max made a mental note opposite - smart girl out-smarted.

"Ah, thanks," she said, "I think."

Max called across to his sisters through the last of the runners, "What was all that about?"

Kira was red-faced, "No idea. Local custom?"

"I'll be Auntie Chloe - sounds cool," beamed Chloe. Kira's look was murderous.

"It's good luck, dear," the woman could see Kira was embarrassed and confused, "To be caught by a whip of one of the priests at the Lupercal Festival means you will be blessed with healthy children."

Lupercal Festival - Max knew it - straight out of "*The noughties*".

"Ah, great," mumbled Kira, "Great."

The runners had passed and the crowd seemed to be following them, pushing closer to the steps where the important Romans were. Kira gestured that they should all follow - most probably to shift the attention from her recent embarrassment. Swallowed by the crowd, the children were swept forward. The cheering was getting louder. Chloe reached for Max's hand, connecting the three siblings in a chain. There was no way they were getting separated here.

The surge pushed them closer to the steps at the far end of the Forum. Suddenly, there he was.

"Great Caesar!" called the lead, goatskin nappy-clad runner as he fell at the feet of the most important Roman. They could now see that this important man - balding, sharp-featured with the name-sake Roman nose and dressed completely in purple robes - was seated centrally on a golden throne and every other Roman was paying him their full attention. This must be the "great" Julius Caesar.

Caesar rose to his feet. "Here is Mark Anthony," he announced. The crowd went wild with cheers and applause as Caesar gave Mark Anthony his hand and made him stand.

Max was amazed. With a wide-eyed expression he turned to his sisters. "That's him," he pointed to Caesar. The crowd stirred around them and all three were pushed further forward still.

"That's who?" asked Chloe.

The crowd erupted again, chanting the name of Caesar over and over. Playing to them, Mark Anthony called out, "Great Caesar, see how the citizens of Rome call your name!"

"That's Julius Caesar," continued Max doing his best to be heard over several hundred excited Romans.

"Who?" mouthed Chloe.

Again a crescendo of recognition spread through the gathered onlookers, "Caesar! Caesar! King of Rome, Caesar for King!"

"Julius Caesar!" Max tried again a little louder.

"Who?"

Max couldn't work it out. Could Chloe not hear him or had she genuinely never heard of Julius Caesar? Kira wasn't listening either. Her eyes were fixed on the action taking place on the steps in front of them. Mark Anthony was now holding a small, golden crown in the air for the benefit of the crowd. "I think they would like Great Caesar to wear this!" he roared.

There was utter pandemonium around them. Hats, aprons, scarves and even a few small children were thrown celebratory-fashion into the air as more extreme applause followed.

"Julius Caesar!" called Max again.

"Who?" Chloe returned again.

"Julius Caesar!" Kira joined in. Mostly through the irritation of listening to Chloe's repeated "who's" that made her sound like a very confused owl.

"Never heard of him," said Chloe matter-of-factly.

"You have," Kira continued, "Everyone has. He was famous."

"She hasn't, you know. He obviously isn't mentioned much in the playground," Max raised his eyes at the general ignorance of six-year-olds.

"You know, Chloe," Kira tried again, "I came, I saw, I conquered."

Chloe shook her head, "Conkers?" There were even louder yells from around them and it seemed that Caesar had turned down the crown once more.

"Mighty Caesar, you disappoint the citizens. They want you as their King!" bellowed Mark Anthony above the cacophony.

Caesar was playing to the crowd now too. "Anthony, you know there is only one King of Rome. Have this crown sent to the Temple of Jupiter. He is King of the Gods and of Rome," he responded.

"Et tu, Brute?" Kira was still trying to get Chloe to appreciate who Caesar was - this time with his famous last words.

"No," Chloe said flatly - clearly not infamous last words then.

Around them, the mood of the crowd was shifting. An air of disappointment was setting in. Their hero, Caesar, had refused his prize.

"Beware the Ides of March?" Kira was desperately seeking a reference for Chloe.

"Sorry?" This was way above Chloe's understanding.

The crowd were unsure now. Some shouted disapproval and others stood and watched as Caesar refused the crown for a third time. The elated mood was falling flat.

"Beware the Ides of March," repeated Kira.

"The eyes of what?"

"The IDES of MARCH!" Kira was getting irritated by her lost cause.

"Ides?" Chloe was very confused.

The crowd's mood lulled as the crown was taken away by one of the priests. It was much calmer now. Caesar was moving away from the throne, waving to supporters and turning to leave with his entourage.

Max, however, had snapped. Oblivious now to the events around him, his patience had evaporated and he barked at Chloe at the top of his lungs, "BEWARE THE IDES OF MARCH!"

Max was aware of a sudden silence around him. People were looking at him. Casear had turned back and was looking in his direction.

"Who calls?" Caesar stood impassive.

Caesar is talking to me, Max thought. *Julius Caesar is talking to me.*

"There is a voice louder than the crowd. Speak again, Caesar is listening," Caesar did not move.

Max was alone now and feeling smaller than his less than average height. The crowd had parted and all eyes were upon him. Kira was mouthing his name whilst shaking her head and even little Chloe was giving a shoulder shrug of embarrassment. Time stood still for Max Foster. Now was the moment that he must talk to Julius Caesar. His mouth dry and his heart pounding, Max turned to meet Caesar's gaze and raised his hand like a guilty schoolboy.

"Beware - the Ides of March," he whispered dryly.

"Who is that?" retorted Caesar.

"A small boy tells you to 'Beware the Ides of March', Caesar," informed a member of Caesar's entourage.

It got even worse for Max. His heart skipped again as he heard Caesar's request, "Bring the boy forward! Let me see him."

Max wasn't sure how he got to stand in front of Julius Caesar in 44 B.C. He couldn't work out if he had been man-handled by the crowd or he had walked trance-like himself. However, there he was on the steps of a marble building in the Roman Forum looking up at Julius Caesar.

"What do you have to say to Caesar now, boy?" Julius glowered down at him.

"Beware - the Ides - of - March," Max was commanded to repeat it - by one of Rome's greatest Generals. He couldn't ignore Julius Caesar. The pause that followed lasted at least a week, Max thought.

Caesar smiled dismissively and turned his gaze to the crowd, "He is a visionary!" Oh, the crowd loved that one. They burst into simultaneous laughter and Max shrank further. "What is your name, boy?"

"Max, Your Emperorness," stuttered Max.

"Maximus, eh?" retorted Caesar and then he turned to the crowd for the killer blow - the remark that would put Max - imus away. "Maximus, here, is a soothsayer!" The crowd loved it. "Come, let us leave, Soothsayer Maximus to his dreams. Come, Anthony. Away! Let us move on."

The whole scene dissolved away around Max. The swathe of the crowd jeered and pointed as they swept slowly by him. Caesar and his entourage strode purposefully ahead of them up the hill towards a large pillared temple. Max stood alone, quietly cringing after what seemed like the whole of the Roman Empire had gathered round for a good laugh at his expense. Kira dragged Chloe across to him.

Max lifted his head and glared at Chloe, his left hand shaking and pointing up the hill towards the temple. *"That's* Julius Caesar!" he spat.

"Hands on history - eh, Maximus," scoffed Kira.

"Not funny," he said.

"Maximus Fosterus. Brother to a marvellous sister, Commander of..."

Max cut through Kira's *Gladiator-style* sarcasm, "Still not funny," he said gesturing his frustration with two outstretched arms and in so doing letting the concealed dagger slip from under his t-shirt and clatter to the floor.

"Nice prediction, young man," said an oily voiced, and rather severe looking, Roman who had sidled over to them. "However, I don't think unsheathed weapons are allowed in the Forum." He stooped to pick up the dagger from Max's feet with a bony hand and smiled a thin smile to his suspicious looking companion. "Especially in the hands of children," he continued, weighing the dagger in his palm. "I had better look after it in case Caesar's Spanish Bodyguard find you with it first." Clenching his fist around the handle the creepy Roman made mock stabbing movements with it then turned his dark gaze to his companion again, "Shall we go, Decimus? The immortal Caesar will be missing us. Let's go and see if he has been promoted to god yet."

The dodgy looking companion gave a wry smile beneath some very neat, dark facial hair. "Very well, Cassius," he smirked. The two sidled away leaving Max and Chloe staring in disbelief but Kira in a clear state of panic.

"He took the dagger," she said seriously.

"Well, he's right, we are children," said Chloe.

"No. He *took the dagger!*" Kira increased the urgency, "*He* took the dagger that killed Julius Caesar."

"But he is still alive," said Max sarcastically, "I just had a *lovely* chat with him."

"All right," said Kira with greater urgency still, "*He* took the dagger that *kills* Julius Caesar on the Ides of March."

"Eh?" said Chloe.

"Ok!" Kira had reached extreme levels of urgency, "The dagger that *kills* Julius Caesar *sometime soon.*"

"Hey, Kira, calm down," urged Max.

"No, Max, I won't calm down! The Roman that took that dagger - the dagger that killed... *kills* Julius Caesar was called Cassius."

"And?" Max had no idea where this Kira tangent moment was going.

"Haven't you learned anything in school?" Kira was really agitated now.

"Of course," said Max, "Just not about Romans."

"OK. OK, listen carefully, Max, I will go very slowly for you," Kira took a deep breath and shook her long hair from her shoulders, "Cassius, the man who took the dagger from you, will become famous. Famous for killing Julius Caesar."

"Wow," Max was impressed by that fact and, with Kira's recollection of it.

"Yeah, Max, wow! And you just gave him the murder weapon!"

Chapter Five

Reality is a very flexible thing when you are little. When you are a toddler, it is perfectly acceptable for animals to talk and little dolls and action figures to have lives of their own but as you grow up, one by one these things become silly and get abandoned. It is a bit like when you first find out there is no Tooth Fairy. Of course, Max would never mention this to Chloe but he found out when he was about eight. His Mother and Father had forgotten to switch one of his 'baby' teeth for the much more easy to spend money the night before and he awoke to the panicked parental conversation of how they would resolve their forgetfulness and preserve the honour of the Tooth Fairy. This was followed by his Dad doing his best to walk nonchalantly to the bathroom and perform a smooth swap as he passed Max's room. He would've succeeded if he hadn't pretended to be tying his shoe laces when Max opened the door to find him kneeling there. I mean, no-one wears shoes to bed!

Max was having reality trouble at this very moment. All the evidence from his current experiences was suggesting he was in Ancient Rome. He was reviewing it now in his head in a *Crimewatch* kind of summary - the warmer climate, the over use of Marble, men wearing short dresses and blankets, definite centurion uniforms, the Forum and a meeting with a man who some may know as Julius Caesar. All perfectly logical so far.

All perfectly logical except for the fact that Max was born in the year 2009 - some two thousand and fifty-three years in the future - in Northampton - some nine hundred and fifty miles from here *and* two thousand and fifty-three years in the future. He had gone on a visit to a National Trust Property setting off about three hours ago but two thousand and sixty-five years in the future.

"Kira, it doesn't make any sense. This can't be happening. It can't be…" Max started to voice his thoughts.

"Real, Max," Kira finished the thoughts off, "This can't be real?"

"It isn't real. It's like…" Chloe couldn't manage it.

"It's like what, Chloe?" Kira thought it was time for some harsh facts, "A dream? A joke? Look around you. Feel the Marble. Catch the sun on your face. It is never this sunny in Northampton and you can't grow a decent crop of olives there either!"

"Tell her, Max," pleaded Chloe.

"He can't, Chloe. He can't explain either. The toga has never been fashionable in Northampton!" Kira was now getting technical in her analysis of Ancient Roman style.

Max was angry. Not because Kira had suggested that he couldn't work it out but because he knew that Kira didn't know what was happening either. If Kira didn't have a solution then something was seriously wrong. After all, what was the point in having a know-it-all big sister if she didn't actually know it all? Who were you supposed to look up to then?

"You think it's real, Kira? You think this is Ancient Rome?" he yelled.

"No. I don't know. I just can't think of a better explanation. Can you?" she yelled back but no one could answer. "And if this is Ancient Rome, we've got to think. We've got to plan. We've got to try to…"

"Get back to Mum and Dad," whispered Chloe.

"And how, Kira? How do we do that?" Max was almost pleading for an explanation.

"I don't know, Max. I don't know. I'm beginning to realise that getting three children and Teddy off a military firing range was a whole lot easier," Kira stopped and thought. "I do have my suspicions though. I really think we should get that dagger back. I think it has something to do with all of this. Somehow. And if all of this is real and this is *hands on history* we have just helped to organise the most famous assassination ever and - that can't be right."

"How do we get it back, Kira?" Max was thinking hard but still having difficulty getting his head around most of the elements of their situation. His head was beginning to hurt.

"I have no idea. You're the soothsayer, Maximus!" she grinned.

"Still not funny, sister," he grinned falsely back.

"What's a soothsayer?" asked Chloe and they all looked at each other.

And then, they laughed. After all, what else can be done in ridiculous and impossible situations but laugh.

"OK, you two, come on," Kira was starting to walk away again.

"Where?" asked Chloe.

"After the togas. To the Capitol," Kira pointed up the hill towards a large and very grand temple.

Max was perplexed. "How come you know so much?" he asked.

"Because," Kira pulled out her 'clever specs' and placed them purposefully on her lightly freckled nose, "I did Romans at school and - I listened." She strode off, knowing neither of her siblings could argue with that; and although Max couldn't see her face, he knew she would be smiling.

Chapter Six

Being typical tourists to Ancient Rome, the Foster children didn't really know where they were going. Max wondered if Kira was tempted to take some photos on her mobile - perhaps a 'selfie' in front of a temple would be *liked* by her three hundred and forty-seven 'friends' - she had never met - on social media? She was striding ahead again and he and Chloe were half running to keep up.

He could see a suitable temple at the top of the hill, directly in front of them. He was sure that one of those monochrome photos taken on a slight angle with her hair swept over her face would look great with that as a backdrop - hundreds of *likes*.

The temple Max was thinking of was, in fact, the most important temple in Rome - the Temple of Jupiter Optimus Maximus. Standing proud at the top of the Capitoline Hill, it had three rows of six enormous, white marble pillars supporting a massive apex roof and guarding the route to the shaded and mysterious inner sanctum. Some of the crowd from the Forum were gathered around the steps, pressing to get another view of Caesar as he appeared from that mysterious inner sanctum.

The children didn't know it on their way up the hill, but the dagger was there too. Cassius and his henchman, Decimus, slid effortlessly into the throng and appeared to be looking for someone. The taller man, Cassius, nodded down to the stocky Decimus to indicate he had spotted that *someone* and, with a renewed purpose, the pair weaved their way through the crowd to reach their target.

A thoughtful looking senator with a serious air stood on the edge of events and was looking at the goings on around the temple with a somewhat confused expression. Marcus Junius Brutus pushed his hand through his short greying hair and shook his head. His face was care worn and deeply jowled - he looked like he hadn't had a decent night's sleep for quite some time. He jumped when he heard a familiar and ominous voice.

"Are you ignoring me, Brutus?" said the fellow senator who had successfully slipped through the crowd to join him.

Brutus was momentarily startled but regained his composure and smiled nervously at the two Romans who had approached him. "No, Cassius."

"Brutus?" Cassius urged with a somewhat sinister smirk to accompany the indifferent cold green eyes.

"I have a lot on my mind," Brutus looked at the polished marble flagstones to avoid his colleague's stares.

"He means the graffiti, Cassius," Decimus hinted.

Brutus was visibly shocked. He was a senator of some renown and had the respect of most in Rome for being a fair and just man but the Brutus family name carried a burden from times past, as they had been the ones who defeated the last of the - most definitely evil - Kings of Rome. "Graffiti?" he asked, lying terribly and in so doing giving away that he knew all about it.

"Come on, Brutus. This is me, Cassius, your brother-in-law. If you need to talk to anyone, you can talk to me," Cassius paused to try to read Brutus' expression, "Everyone has seen the graffiti. The message is clear."

"Cassius, no!" Brutus was clearly uncomfortable with where this conversation was going. "This is dangerous talk," he pleaded.

"And these are dangerous times, Brutus. Men are looking for guidance; for a strong leader; for another of the famous Brutus family to rise up like all those years ago," Cassius was cut short as a raucous cheer broke from the crowd again. The ever athletic Mark Anthony had emerged from the depths of the temple and was leading Caesar's entourage towards them.

Brutus' expression softened, relieved by the distraction. He changed the subject, "The dedication has finished. Caesar is leaving the temple."

"As they pass, Brutus, stop Casca. He'll tell us what happened in there," insisted Cassius, his hand twisting agitatedly on the pommel of the dagger he had taken from Max.

Somewhat too loudly, Max spotted Cassius and the dagger as he and his two sisters arrived, a little breathless, at the top of the Hill. "There he is!" he yelled, "He's got the dagger!"

Some of the crowd turned to stare and Max shrugged his shoulders uncomfortably to dismiss their attention. Fortunately for him, Cassius and Decimus seemed not to have heard and carried on talking.

"What do we do?" asked Chloe.

"What about - 'Hey, Mister, can we have our lethal dagger back to play with?'" Max answered sarcastically.

"D'ya think?" said Chloe - with quite a put down for a six-year-old.

"Stop it, you two. Let's get a little closer. Find out who they are talking to and think of something," Kira was always the voice of reason and they moved closer. She gestured for them to stop when they were a few crowd members away. Cassius and Decimus were talking with some urgency to an important looking man. He seemed uncomfortable; looking around with sad blue eyes as if to check no one was listening to what was being said. A sudden loud fanfare parted the crowd and Caesar's procession made their way past - preceded and followed by those menacing soldiers in full armour. Max hid. He could feel his face burning up and knew he must be a ridiculous shade of red. Concealing himself behind the broadest Roman available should prevent him from accidentally making any more prophecies, he thought.

The procession passed and Max looked back to see what Cassius was doing. Now, he had been joined by another important looking Roman - a short and rather round man with a face redder than Max's embarrassment and blonde hair that looked like it had been cut around the rim of a saucepan. Max turned back to speak to Kira but she wasn't there. After the crowd had parted, she had taken advantage of the situation and moved closer to Cassius and the dagger. Max squeezed past the broad Roman in front of him to get to her. He could just about hear Cassius' conversation as he addressed the stout, red-faced man.

"But what happened, Casca?" Cassius urged.

"You were there, weren't you?" said red-faced Casca.

"Would I be asking you if I were?" Cassius' patience was failing quickly.

"You weren't at the dedication?" Casca spluttered, rather pompously.

"We arrived late," added Brutus.

"Late?" Casca snorted and his ample cheeks wobbled.

"Yes, Casca, late," Cassius really wanted Casca to get to the point and he resorted to sharp sarcasm, "Delayed by a multiple chariot pile-up on the Appian Way."

Casca missed the joke and instead looked for any gossip, "Really? Anyone injured?"

"Just tell us what happened, Casca," this time, there was no mistaking Cassius' reply. It was almost a threat and Casca looked worried - as if he knew that Cassius were not to be messed with. Casca quickly got on with recounting what he had seen.

"Well, it was the crown that Mark Anthony offered him at the Rostra - You know - that gold one. Not really a crown, more sort of a coronet or a tiara: nice though; jewels; good quality; and must've cost a bit." Casca became aware, from Cassius' glare, that his audience weren't really interested in the finer appreciation of regal headgear - just the facts. He continued, "He pretended not to be interested in it -"

"Pretended?" asked Brutus.

"Oh, he wanted it, Brutus. I think -" Casca looked around him furtively, "- I think he wants to be King."

"King?" Brutus was horrified - as if something big and very bad were about to happen.

"Of Rome," continued Casca, "He gave the crown to the statue of Jupiter to make himself look humble!" Casca huffed his disapproval of such an obvious tactic and his thoughts turned, as they often did, to food, "Well, gentlemen, if that is all, I have a dozen baked dormice awaiting my attention." He rubbed his extended stomach in anticipation and shook hands with the other three before saying his farewells and puffing away after the procession.

"They eat dormice?" shrieked Chloe.

"Mmm, small but satisfying!" Max received a kick from a distraught Chloe - dormice were far too cute to eat.

Cassius was raging now, "Just who does he think he is, some kind of giant? Does Julius Caesar really have superhuman powers?"

Brutus shifted agitatedly, "Careful, Cassius, he has friends everywhere."

"But he's just a man, Brutus. A man like you," Cassius put his arm around Decimus' broad shoulders and drew him in, "Or Decimus. Or me. He is only mortal and he can bleed." Cassius pulled out the confiscated dagger and held it out in front of him. Brutus' jaw dropped in horror. The children stared in frustration, somehow knowing they needed to get that dagger back.

Brutus knew he needed to conceal it. "Cassius, what are you thinking? Why have you brought your dagger? Do you want to be arrested?" Brutus flung the left sleeve of his toga over Cassius' outstretched arm to hide the weapon.

"It isn't mine," said Cassius, "I, err, confiscated it from some children." Cassius smiled his oily smile.

"It wouldn't matter if it was your dead Mother's best asparagus knife, brother in law. If Caesar's Spanish Guard see you armed -"

he paused, "You aren't a soldier any more, Cassius." Brutus stopped again to compose himself, "Come on. My house is close by. We will leave that dagger there. Come on. You too, Decimus. Keep it hidden, Cassius and come on."

Brutus bundled the lean figure of Cassius before him and gestured for Decimus to follow. Swiftly and effectively, the three left the Capitoline Hill and the dagger was taken out of reach once more. This time, it was going to the house of Brutus - wherever that may be.

"Oh, great," sighed Max stepping from behind a group of onlookers, "We've lost it again!"

Kira had been quiet for a very long time. She had clearly been thinking again. She looked down at Max and removed her glasses with her right hand, stabbing the air with them as she spoke, "Right, you two, listen." Kira looked amazed to have received no argument from her brother and sister and so continued, "If this is Ancient Rome - and I'm beginning to think it really has to be - we do actually have some advantages over everyone else here."

"Eh?" was all Max could manage - a statement that was a few centuries of evolution short of eloquent.

Kira carried on, "Think, Max - we are currently in Rome over two thousand years before we actually got up this morning. We are from the future."

"We come in peace!" Max couldn't resist his best Star Trek impression.

"Max! Just listen. We know everything that's going to happen here. We know exactly what events will take place because, to us, they have already taken place and - luckily, one of us has read a history book." The clever specs were back on again now and Max had a horrible feeling that Kira was about to show off again. "We know that Julius Caesar was assassinated," she stated then caught the confused expression of little Chloe and corrected herself, "Killed. Killed on the Ides of March."

"What is the Ides of March, Kira?" Chloe was having trouble

keeping up already.

"It is a specific day in March - I think it is the 15th but I'd need to check." Max was about to have a dig about Googling it but decided that if Kira really did have a plan, it was probably best to listen carefully. She went on, "We know that today is the 15th February, thanks to Mr. Sabre in the Market Place, and we know there is some kind of festival today."

"That's right!" chipped in Chloe, "The feast of Calpol."

It would have been too cruel to pick little Chloe up on this one, so Max and Kira glanced at each other and made the joint decision to let that one go - the Feast of Calpol it would now become. Kira returned to the facts, "I remember that Caesar received a warning from a soothsayer to 'Beware the Ides of March' and it seems that, thanks to Maximus providing the prediction, we are now actively involved in the events leading up to Caesar's death."

"You mean I am the soothsayer. The real historical one! Cool! Wow!" Max was quickly sliding from historical to hysterical.

"Well, yes. It fits with recorded events - with the real historic account studied by millions of students worldwide. Some who even listen and remember, Max. It also seems that we have innocently provided the murder weapon by giving our dagger to a known assassin - Cassius."

"How can you say that, Kira?" Max jibed.

"I can't say anything for definite. But then again, when I woke up this morning - on your average, grey and wet October day in Northampton - I didn't say to myself, 'I know, I think I will visit Ancient Rome today!'" Max fell silent - well and truly put in his place. "Everything seems to revolve around the dagger that we brought here. We were warned, by Sir Walter, not to take anything but we did - maybe accidentally but nevertheless - we did take something and we brought it here somehow. I'm beginning to think *it* brought us here somehow. However it happened, that dagger is now in the hands of the men who, according to every Historian since - well, since here and now, - killed the most famous Roman of them all."

"Julius Caesar," whispered Chloe, not really expecting to be right.

"That's right, Chloe. And, we have become involved. We've got to get un-involved. We must get that dagger back because," Kira paused as she was about to deliver the hardest part of her developing theory to swallow, the hardest because even she wasn't sure, "I think it will get us home. Somehow."

Somehow was the word of the moment. It perfectly reflected their situation. If they were honest, no-one had the slightest idea how they seemed to have gone from the polished oak of stately Britain to the smooth marble of Rome on the verge of Empire.

"You keep going back to that, Kira. How can a dagger get us home?" Max was showing his frustration.

"Well, Maximus, *if* we get it back, I will be able to see if I am right."

From a little brother with a know-it-all sister point-of-view, Max hoped she was wrong so he could have hours of fun telling her how ridiculous her theory had been; but, from a little boy wanting to be back with Mum and Dad in the correct time and place point-of-view, he hoped to goodness that she had a point.

In the perfect impression of her sister of eight years superiority, Chloe was striding off down the hill. "Come on then," she called, "They took it this way."

"I'm sure it was this way," said Max, setting off in the opposite direction.

Kira was in the middle. After a moment's pause she turned and followed Chloe. "No offence, Max," she called, "You don't listen so you probably don't look either."

Max stood open mouthed. Not for long though as very quickly, he was following his sisters again.

Chapter Seven

Kira was right - there was never this much sun in Northampton *and* the three of them had dressed for October. Chloe and Max were without cardigan and hoodie respectively - having removed them to try on historical items but thick jeans, boots and trainers were proving very sticky. For a very brief moment, Max considered the 1950's, knitted, three-quarter length shorts that his Mum was planning for him. No. Not even two thousand and sixty-five years in the past, a thousand miles from home and in a city where men wore dresses and blankets would he attempt that kind of dress-sense suicide. He was often told by Kira that he didn't think about his appearance enough. Admittedly, he didn't get up two hours before school to shower, blow dry and straighten his hair and apply as much make up as he could possibly get away with on the off chance that a certain, special person may be on the school bus that day - like she did - but, he knew enough about fashion to know that woollen shorts were just - wrong. Very wrong. What was his mum thinking of?

What was his Mum thinking of right now? Had she noticed he was missing? Had she wondered if he and his sisters had wandered off? Well, they certainly had wandered off and right now, all three of them would have given anything not to have opened that closed door with that sign - 'No Entry'. Max thought of one of his Dad's favourite sayings - that 'hindsight was a wonderful thing'. He had heard his Dad say it umpteen times over the years and thought recently it was probably a good idea to find out what on earth he was on about - so he asked. Apparently, it meant that when things turned out not quite as you expected (usually negatively), it was all very well wishing you had done things differently but at the time you made the choices, you didn't expect a bad result. Looking back and knowing how things turned out couldn't change the past - hindsight was, therefore, pointless.

Except that it wasn't. If Kira, Chloe and Max were in Ancient

Rome, they had the most incredible gift to offer. They could go up to Julius Caesar and tell him. They could 'shop' Cassius and Decimus and have them arrested. They could save Julius Caesar by insisting he take a last minute holiday a few days before The Ides of March. They could change history.

Hindsight could change the course of events and they had the power to keep Julius Caesar alive by telling him what they knew would happen. Of course, Max would have to get the facts of the story checked by Kira first but once he had got them right, he could make one massive difference. That was if anyone would listen to a small boy publicly labelled a dreamer by History's most influential Roman.

Kira grabbed his arm really hard and Max yelped out of his thoughts. She was trying to stop him walking right into the three Romans they had been trying to find. Cassius, Decimus and Brutus had arrived at the grand, olive grove shaded gates of a villa and were being greeted by a slim, smiling lady in an ivory dress - her long, dark hair held back by a small gold headband. This must be Brutus' wife. Again, the three found themselves trying to hide and the low white-washed wall of a neighbouring villa did the job. They peered from behind it. Chloe looked around the edge as she wasn't tall enough.

"Caius Cassius, here again, no notice as usual, " the woman was saying.

"You know me, Portia, everything on the spur of the moment. Thinking too much doesn't get things done." Cassius grinned suggestively.

"But always welcome," she continued, "You too Decimus."

"Thank you, Portia," Decimus bowed his head gratefully.

Portia turned to Brutus. "How was the Festival of the Lupercal?" she asked.

"Predictable," said Brutus, agitatedly. He seemed keen to get his two guests off the street and into the villa - out of sight.

"You mean Mark Anthony won?" laughed Portia.

"Oh, he's so masculine!" Cassius laughed.

Brutus gestured for Portia to lead them in and was the last to go through the gates - stopping to take one last and worried look down his very quiet street. Max appeared from behind the wall, still hurting from Kira's restraining grab. "I mean it's not like going to ask for our ball back!" he exploded.

"I know," Kira stood up.

"Please can we have it back? We promise not to stab anyone," his rant went on.

"I know."

"We are really well-adjusted young people with a healthy interest in antique daggers - that's all," Max had snapped - maybe it was sun stroke. He had woken up this morning much further away from the equator than he was now and it must have had a disorientating effect.

"I know. Any sensible ideas?"

"No, Kira, I've never stolen anything before," he was still too hot under the collar to have ideas.

"My money box," Chloe stated. She could really stop a rant when she wanted to.

"You didn't?" said Kira, genuinely shocked.

"Borrowed," spluttered Max, "That money was borrowed."

"Mum got it back, Kira, it's OK," Chloe re-assured her big sister.

"Borrowed," whined Max but, realising that two girls would always side with each other over the word of an insignificant boy, he changed the subject. "Anyway, how do we get in?" Max pointed to Brutus' large, wooden villa gates.

"We could go over the wall," suggested Chloe.

"We're not ninjas," laughed Max.

"Then we will go over at night," said Kira like it was the most ordinary thing to do - breaking and entering, trespassing and finally a spot of stealing for good measure.

Max's mind was racing again, "What if they have dogs? Big dogs! Did the Romans have big dogs?"

"Ah, Max," said Kira tapping the side of her nose wisely, "If only you had listened in those History lessons, then you would know if you were going to get bitten or not."

"Me?"

"You're a boy," Chloe's argument was certainly grounded in fact.

"Great," he said, "Who would be a boy?"

Then, there was one of those silences where nothing was actually said but so much was decided. It dawned on all of them that it would be Max attempting to get the dagger back but that none of them knew how long it would be until darkness fell. Max broke the silence, "Right, so what do we do until it gets dark then?"

"Max, this is Ancient Rome," Kira pleaded - then just to make sure added, "Probably."

Max said nothing, waiting for Kira to suggest something.

"I mean, it is incredible," she enthused, "So much to see and do. So much to experience and tell people about when we get back."

"Oh, yeah. Cool," said Max, "And then we can all get sectioned."

Two elderly Roman ladies had appeared at a nearby gate. From their conversation, it was clear that one had spent the afternoon visiting the other and was just going home. They didn't seem to notice the children.

"And so I said to him, 'What's the point having hypocaust if you're not going to use it?' I mean it was freezing last night," said the lady leaving as she adjusted her headscarf and multi-layered rose-pink gown.

"Oh, I know," said the owner of the house.

"And, we've just had it re-tiled. New mosaics - lovely."

"Oh, I know."

The children stood and listened.

"And the cost - hundreds of Dinaris."

"Oh, I know."

"Anyway, I can't stop chatting any longer, see you at the Circus Maximus, Julia. Bye."

"Bye, Augusta, bye," she waved her friend down the street then smiling to the youngsters, she went back into her villa.

"Not so different," smiled Chloe.

"What?" asked Max.

"Ancient Rome isn't so different. Those two were just like Nan." Chloe had a point.

"Yes," said Kira, "They were." Kira looked kindly at her little sister and crouched down to her level, "I'll get us back home you know."

"I know," nodded Chloe.

"And the journey home starts with Maximus here getting over this wall," Kira turned to Max to see his worried expression. "Come on, Max. What's the worst that could happen?" she asked.

"Oh, you know, dogs. Those big dogs," Max panicked, "Lions! The Romans kept lions."

"Yes, Max, but not in their front gardens. You just have to get over the wall and see if you can find the dagger. Then we can all go home," Kira smiled, "Maybe."

"You do realise that this is emotional blackmail," Max complained.

"Of course," said Kira, "And sisters are experts at it."

Chapter Eight

Some things are worth the wait - like birthdays or Christmas or the burger without relish that they have to cook specially for you. Other things - like the Dentist, injections and Dad's bizarre chocolate chilli con carne should never have existed, let alone be waited for. The rest of the afternoon in Ancient Rome was a mixture of the two - a series of exciting and unbelievable experiences that filled a gap leading towards a necessary nasty.

For instance, Max had been challenged in the street by a real centurion to play a bizarre board game with counters and dice - and all because he had loudly suggested that the game that was being played looked like draughts; and draughts was easy. Amazingly, though not understanding the rules at all and receiving absolutely no support from his mortified sisters, he had won a few games. Kira had been shopping and, in spite of Max's hopeless jokes about going to *T. K. Maximus*, had managed to barter her modern jewellery for some beautiful glass beads. Roman glass beads from 44 B.C. - now that was incredible. And, Chloe, well, she had made some genuine Ancient Roman friends by getting involved in a game of Leap Frog in the Market Place with locals of her own age. On saying goodbye to Marcus, Sophia and Lysander, it had taken all Kira's effort not to cry when Chloe had said that she couldn't wait to come back on holiday to Ancient Rome again next year and play some more. Max was just glad that she had never heard of penpals.

However, all good things must end as they say and, an ending of sorts had definitely come for this day. It was dusk and time to attempt to get that dagger back in the hope that Kira had some kind of theory. They had worked their way back in the gathering darkness to Brutus' villa and were sat on the low wall that they had hidden behind earlier.

"Ready, Max?" asked Kira, "I'll give you a leg up."

"Oh, great," muttered Max as he stood up and walked to the villa wall. Kira knelt and cupped her hands to hold and lift his foot. Would she toss him over caber-like and into the open mouths of big Roman dogs like some Amphitheatre version of the Highland Games? No, she needed him alive to get the dagger to go home to update *Instachat* or something. Max grizzled at her and took the leg up, scrambling nimbly to the ridge of the wall. He turned back to look down at his sisters and show them that he may well have been a ninja in a previous life; and - promptly lost his balance, disappearing quickly as gravity took a hold. There was a large crash like breaking flower pots and a not insignificant, "Ouch!" from Max.

Kira scrambled up the wall and held on, peering over to find that Max had suffered a collision with a large, white statue. He looked up at her, waving the statue's broken arm in a 'what do I do now?' sort of a way.

Kira couldn't resist, "Told you, Max, Romans are totally 'armless'!"

"You're not helping," he whispered. Chloe, Of course, couldn't see and was repeatedly asking if Max was OK. Kira turned to give her a thumbs up to indicate that the only thing broken was a statue.

Max could hear voices. Someone was definitely coming this way and on his side of the wall.

"Lucius. Lucius! Wine, Lucius. Wine to the orchard, Lucius!" it was Brutus' wife, Portia, calling. Max looked around him. There were trees everywhere and he would have put money on every single one of them being a fruit tree. Kira sensed people coming too and gestured for Max to hide.

'Where?" he mouthed to her but all she could do was shrug her shoulders and tap the side of her head to suggest that he used his initiative.

There are moments in life when good choices, decisions or moves are made - this was not one of those moments. In fact,

Max could hear his Dad's quote about hindsight loud and clear and ringing in his ears. He could see the light of an oil lamp approaching accompanied by conversation that was getting louder and he needed to do something quickly. He hid behind the statue, holding the arm back in, what he thought was, the right place.

To the young servant boy of Brutus and Portia - Lucius - who appeared from the darkness of the trees with a lamp, amphora and goblets, the statue looked like it had done fourteen rounds with Agrippa - Rome's best Gladiator - and lost every single one. Lucius did not think it was possible to dislocate your arm so horrifically and whilst pouring the wine and setting the lamp into an alcove in the wall above a garden seat, he stared at the statue - transfixed. Portia and Cassius joined him and continued their conversation on the seat. All the while, Lucius seemed to be getting closer to Max's hiding place and, to add to the tension, the arm of the statue was getting very heavy.

"To the Republic." Portia raised her goblet of wine.

"Should it last." Cassius cynically raised his and they clinked a toast.

"Always such a negative future with you, Cassius." Portia drank slowly, her eyes on Cassius all the time.

"On the contrary, sister, I am a realist. It will end much sooner than you think. Change is coming; and very soon." He drank deeper and gave the impression that he knew something.

Lucius was getting too close. Max would be visible if he took another five steps towards him.

"You're paranoid, Cassius."

Four steps.

"We'll see, Sister."

Now three steps.

"Brutus seems well, though," Cassius had changed the subject.

Just two steps.

"Caesar's pardon still hangs heavy on him. He has too big a conscience."

And one step.

"The people love him for that, sister."

Smack. Max had no choice but to hit him with it. With one swing of the statue's broken arm, Lucius was out cold.

"Did you hear something, Portia?" Cassius had risen and was looking into the night gloom as Max skilfully juggled the statue's arm whilst supporting the slumped, unconscious servant boy.

"Probably just Lucius. He can be a bit clumsy," replied Portia.

"Or Brutus and Decimus knocking something over with those huge scrolls they are still looking at." Both Cassius and Portia laughed.

Out on the street outside, Kira had been holding Chloe up to the wall at arms length - like a small human periscope - to try to discover what was happening to Max.

"Incoming!" Chloe shouted - wriggling free from Kira's grip to take cover as a white plaster arm flew over the wall from the orchard. Then, more bizarrely still, a human hand appeared at the wall, waving strangely - limply, as if with a broken wrist. Assuming it was Max, Kira scrambled up the wall, grabbed at the hand and pulled. A small figure came back with her, landing square on top of her as they tumbled to the floor.

"Max! You -" Kira broke off. A small fair-haired boy, probably about the same age as Max and dressed in a light brown tunic and sandals, appeared to be asleep on her. She pushed him off and scrambled to her feet, dusting down her clothes and staring at the stranger who looked very peaceful in his unconsciousness. Chloe joined her for a stare. There was a scrabbling from behind them and the girls turned to see Max fall from the top of the wall and back into the street with them. There was no way that he could get away with describing that exit as stealth-like.

"Excellent," started Kira, "Not content with predicting the murder of the most important Roman of them all *and* providing the murder weapon - Kira, Max and Chloe advance their criminal activities to KIDNAPPING!"

"Sssh," Max tried to draw Kira's attention to the fact that they were only a few metres from Brutus' garden where Romans were still out and about.

"What next, Max?" Kira ignored his pleas, "Extortion?"

"I can do that," said Chloe and she started to pull bizarre facial expressions. Max was puzzled.

"That's contortion, Chloe." Kira had worked it out.

"I knew that," Chloe lied.

"What are we going to do with him?" hissed Kira, still angry at their situation which was now spiraling even further out of their control.

"Can we keep him?" asked Chloe.

"He's not a pet, Chloe!" Kira had lost all patience now.

"We can make him get the dagger for us," reasoned Max.

"That *is* extortion, Max." Kira shot him a look of total impatience now.

"Ask him to get the dagger for us then," Max tried again.

"Slightly better," Kira stopped talking as Lucius made a low groan from the floor.

"What do we say to him, Max?" Chloe asked.

Max didn't have a clue. He was so far out of his comfort zone that he was losing touch with his already slim grasp of their current 'reality' - again. After all, he had just hit a Roman servant with the plaster arm of a statue and knocked him out - yet another out-of-the-ordinary event in an extraordinary day. He decided to take charge. He would show his sisters how he was in control of the situation. Striding to Lucius, who was stirring on the floor, he stood with arms crossed and said -

"Hi."

What brilliant eloquence - that would make everything clear. He tried again, "Err, I am Max - imus." Max offered his hand to the boy but Lucius had started to shuffle away from him on his hands, feet and backside. Realising that the servant boy thought Max was going to hit him again, he continued, "Sorry. This one is real. Feel." Lucius tentatively took Max's hand and was helped to his feet. "This is my big sister, Kira and my little sister, Chloe," Max added.

"Sorry about the kidnapping," Chloe apologised and both Max and Kira gave her looks to be quiet.

"Lucius," said the boy in the tunic.

"Lucius," repeated Max, "Cool."

"No, Lucius Martius," corrected the confused servant boy.

There was no time for the finer points of cultural linguistic differences. Max decided to cut to the chase, "So, Lucius, you're a slave then?"

"Oh, subtle," groaned Kira.

Lucius, however, looked comfortable enough with this title, saying, "Yes, Maximus. My master is Marcus Brutus." Lucius was pointing to Brutus' villa to indicate where he lived.

"And does he have a big knife?" chipped in Chloe, innocently, "Cos if he does it's ours and he stole it."

Clearly aware that this situation was in need of a level-headed, sophisticated approach, Kira stepped in to explain, "I'm sorry, Lucius, but what my simple siblings are trying to get at is that when we arrived in Rome, earlier today, Cassius - a friend of your Master, I believe - took a dagger from us."

"And we need it to get back home," added Max naively.

Kira continued to put things right, providing the correct amount of spin for their story to get it accepted by Lucius, "We need to *put* it back *in* our home. In our *Cabinet of sentimental trophies.* It has unbelievable value. Sentimentally, you understand?"

Lucius understood and held up his wrist on which he wore a rough looking copper bracelet. "Like this," he said.

Chloe did not understand and put her hands on her hips to correct him. "Well, our dagger is bigger; and shinier; and, most likely, much more expensive; and obviously much better made."

"It was given to me by my mother," Lucius continued, "Before she was killed."

Chloe got it this time. "And not as valuable as that beautiful bracelet you are wearing, Lucius," she lied as an almost successful apology.

There was an out-pouring of emotion from the Foster children. Missing their parents after just a few hours - all be it two thousand and sixty-five years on a chronological timeline sort of a way - had made all three of them appreciate the often moaned about and never appreciated Mum and Dad. Max tried to apologise for knocking Lucius out with the statue arm, explaining that he was really just trying to hide and Kira gave a direct apology for not realising Lucius was an orphan.

"It was long ago," Lucius explained, "She was killed whilst working in the fields and I was captured." Lucius paused then continued, "And sold as a slave." He twisted the copper bracelet lovingly as the three children watched in awe of the composure of this little servant boy and his powerful and truly sad story. "I understand sentimental value. We will get your special blade back," he finished.

Everyone's mood lifted - Kira, Max and Chloe because they had a glimmer of hope of a return to their everyday life and Lucius because he seemed to have found new and definitely very different friends.

"It is getting late; the household will be asleep soon. The guests are staying here tonight," Lucius started to outline what he thought should be done. "I must get back to the house. They will want more wine before they retire for the night. Maximus, you could help. Come back with me and keep a look out whilst I retrieve your knife from Cassius' bedchamber."

Max knew that after knocking him unconscious a few moments ago, he couldn't really justify saying no to Lucius and shrugged his shoulders in what came across as extremely mild agreement.

"And Chloe and me?" asked Kira.

"You ladies should stay here," said Lucius with genuine care.

"Yeah, Max," taunted Chloe, "Us ladies should stay here. Off you go."

Yet again, Max found himself at the wall of Brutus' villa and this time he was offering to give a genuine Roman slave a leg up. Could the day possibly get any more surreal?

Lucius paused on top of the wall. "We will get the dagger," he said with a smile and he jumped quietly into the orchard.

Max was scrambling after him. "Yeah, don't worry about us," he said as he fell face first off the wall and into the garden. Kira and Chloe winced as they heard the thump of his less than stealthy landing. "I'm OK," Max lied in a pain-concealing and very forced whisper.

Chapter Nine

Even at the very advanced age of *nearly twelve*, the darkness of night can still hold a few worries. Max, for example - who was absolutely the very advanced age of *nearly twelve* - was terrified of the dark. When Mum and Dad had received, what they had called, 'the electricity bill for Blackpool Illuminations', one of their money saving schemes had been to turn off the landing light as soon as the children were in bed. Max remembered the palpitations he had had as he heard this plan. What kind of savage parents would plunge their innocent babes into the obvious dangers of a pitch black family home for the endless length of an entire night? Anything could happen. What if one of the posters fell from his wall to the floor or a floorboard creaked, or the radiators ticked as they cooled for the night? How would he not let his imagination run away with itself when he couldn't see to provide a logical explanation to stop it?

Things got so desperate that, in a bid to discover if he was going mad, because he was sure he had turned off the light, Dad stood halfway up the stairs in that deadly darkness and caught Max in the act of creeping to the landing light switch to turn it back on.

There was a particular type of darkness surrounding Max now - a particularly creepy one. The orchard trees appeared gnarled and twisted in a very dim moonlight and every single one of them seemed to be leaning in his direction - as if to make a grab for him. What made things worse was that a slight breeze had got up and was making them move. Max had never appreciated the warm glow of twenty-first century street lamps as much as he did now. They would certainly have provided enough light to sort these trees out.

Lucius had been gone ages. Once Max had regained some feeling in his legs after his graceless fall back into Brutus' garden, he had remained hidden behind the statue and received the occasional progress report regarding the bedtime preparations of Brutus, Portia and their guests. When they had finally gone to bed, Max had been left to guard the back door. What Lucius expected to surprise him at the back door, Max wasn't sure - he really hoped Lucius didn't know something about these creepy trees that he wasn't letting on.

There was a sudden flurry of movement and Lucius burst through the back entrance of the villa in such fury that it made Max jump. He was coming at some speed and carrying something. There was commotion too - noises were coming from the villa. The household was waking up. Lucius skidded to a halt, level with Max. He was carrying the dagger and he was very breathless.

"Come on, Maximus," he panted, "Cassius is awake."

It had to be the sinister one, didn't it? The one whose steely gaze and oily manner would unnerve the bravest Roman of them all. The one who clearly had connections with some sort of violent revolutionary uprising. It couldn't be Portia, the gentle lady of the house, or the reasonable and mild mannered Brutus - it had to be the suspicious looking and obviously slightly unhinged, Cassius. Max sprang after Lucius who was heading away from the wall and through the fruit trees.

"Lucius!" Max called, "The wall! Kira and Chloe are over the other side."

"I know," shouted Lucius, "I'm going to the back gate."

'There is a back gate?' thought Max as he made a mental note of the injuries sustained from three drops from the perimeter wall as the victim of gravity. Before he could extend his list from bruises to scratches, they were at a large gate set into an archway within the plastered wall. Lucius was pulling at the gate as Cassius' silhouette had appeared in the back doorway of the villa. Max looked back and could just make out his angry features highlighted in silver moonlight whilst he hastily adjusted his toga.

Brutus was on the move too. "What, Lucius? What, in the

name of all the gods at once, is going on?" he called.

"There," yelled Cassius, pointing at them both, "Lucius has taken the dagger. The dagger I got from those children in the market place. There he is. Look! And, I swear that is that soothsayer boy from the Forum - Maximus!"

They left the house and were heading towards the two boys, covering ground at an alarming rate with determined adult strides. Decimus was there too, rubbing sleep from his eyes and cursing about having too much wine. This was a situation that could end really badly. Max found that he was actually deciding which of his pursuers he would chance sticking the dagger into; and that definitely could not be right.

In the street outside, Chloe was leaning against her sister. Uncomfortable she may have been but she was most definitely asleep. Her wide brown eyes had lost the battle to stay awake and her little round head was snuggled into Kira's side. Kira smiled at Chloe's little sleep murmurings, realising that Chloe was still very small. Kira was tired too and looked very sleepy. Her eyes closed - only to be snapped open instantly in reaction to a loud scraping sound, fast footsteps and the appearance of two much-panicked boys a little further up the road. Kira stirred Chloe from her sleep as Max and Lucius had skidded into the lane.

"Guess they weren't asleep then?" Kira joked to Max.

"No," yelled Max, "On the plus side, we found no ferocious lions - but we did attract some pretty angry Romans. I say we run. Now!"

Kira could see Lucius had the dagger; she could hear the commotion in the orchard but there were other noises. Approaching behind Lucius and Max was a small group of what appeared to be Roman soldiers. Kira didn't stop to find out for sure, grabbing Chloe's little hand, she ran, dragging her sleepy sister away from the villa as the group of Roman soldiers arrived at Brutus' back gate. Max and Lucius sprinted to the girls and the group of children ran for their lives together.

There were four soldiers - all muscle-bound and bristling for some kind of action. The platoon leader stepped forward, removing his plumed helmet to address Cassius. He was square jawed, with close-cropped hair and his eyebrows met in the middle to give him a very intense expression - rather like he was visually concentrating that little bit too hard.

"What is all this commotion so late? We'll have no trouble here," he ordered, stopping Cassius from pursuing the children with an outstretched hand that was the size of a shovel. Brutus wasn't far behind Cassius now and Decimus and even Portia had arrived on the street.

"Brutus, what has happened? What is going on?" Portia asked her husband.

"Calm yourself, Madam. I am fully trained in conflict management and have opened a dialogue with this citizen to identify the cause of this urban disturbance," the centurion announced, gripping Cassius more firmly.

"Lucius has taken the dagger," hissed Cassius in a clear rage from the indignation of being squeezed by a centurion.

"Lucius, sir? Might I enquire who that would be?" asked the centurion, clearly following some sort of investigative procedure.

"Our slave," answered Portia.

The centurion paused. From his eyebrow movement, you could see the thought processes as a physical act. He spun round to address his tiny platoon dragging the tightly gripped Cassius with him. "Ah, slaves rebellion, troops! There will be crucifixions on the Appian Way soon enough," the centurion laughed throwing his hands aloft and Cassius to the floor.

"Slave, not slaves," interjected a bemused Brutus as he stepped forward to offer the dishonoured Cassius his hand.

"But armed you say? With a dagger?" The centurion was clearly keen to establish the facts. His eyebrow lowered and he squinted his dark eyes, dangerously. "We may need back up, boys," he called to his troops who could be seen tightening their grips on their shields and sword pommels.

"He's ten years old," added Portia.

The centurion thought again for a moment - just as painfully as before. "Low level assault, eh?" he mused.

"Stop this. Stop this nonsense," interjected Cassius, who was now up and dusted down, as the small platoon prepared not to take any notice and move out. "Halt!" Cassius yelled at the top of his voice. That had the desired effect and everyone stopped in their tracks.

The centurion strode to Cassius menacingly and, with his face mere centimetres from him, said suspiciously, "Military training, eh? This conflict situation gets more and more complex."

"Conflict situation?" queried Brutus, "What *conflict situation?*"

Portia stepped in, "Our ten-year-old slave, Lucius, has merely taken a sword and run away. He may be with other *children*. That is hardly an excuse for a war footing. Couldn't you just bring him back?"

"Bring him back?" the centurion puzzled over the words slowly. "Bring him back. Oh, I see, for interrogation with the implements of torture."

"No," Brutus cut in, alarmed.

"Severe beating then?" the centurion sounded like he was making a request.

"Certainly not," cried Portia.

"Minor beating - no noticeable bruises?" the centurion asked.

"No beating," Decimus clarified; breaking his bemused silence, "Just apprehend him, please."

"What if he mounts a retaliation?"

The centurion's question had fallen on incredulous ears and wide mouthed expressions were the look of choice.

"He is ten years old," repeated Portia.

"Ye gods, how I miss the front line," the centurion pleaded, starry-eyed, "Platoon, seek, locate and," he paused to be greeted by unimpressed looks from Brutus, Portria and their guests, "Gently restrain." The centurion was clearly disappointed.

With one final, very over-complicated, hand gesture, the troops were in hot pursuit. It had been a long time since the platoon leader had had anything troublesome to deal with and he was going to make absolutely sure that he exaggerated this event out of all proportion to get the most out of this bit of action.

Chapter Ten

Max imagined street lamps again - they really were the best invention Max could think of at the moment. Navigating the twisting back streets of Ancient Rome at night and at high speed, would definitely have been much easier with that friendly night glow from the future. Here in the past, the narrow alleys were full of unseen obstacles to fall over or in to. The four children - now including Lucius, the genuine Roman slave - were ricocheting from pillar to chariot rut and bouncing off hazardously parked carts and lazily placed crates and barrels. They had the dagger and now needed to try Kira's theory of finding the exact place they arrived at - without the aid of street lamps.

Adding to the stress of their situation, they were now well aware that they were being chased. The Roman soldiers, that had arrived at the house of Brutus as the children had made their escape, suddenly seemed very keen to talk to them. They also seemed to be able to run much faster and definitely had the advantage of a superior local knowledge. Max made a mental note to ask Mum and Dad for gym equipment for his twelfth birthday so as to get fit enough not to be embarrassingly outrun by historical figures should he meet any in the future. That would, of course, be any *future* trips to - the *past*. How complicated it was to make reference to time when one was a time-traveller.

The alley they were currently stumbling down ended abruptly in a T-junction.

"Where now?" urged Kira.

To their left, a similar, narrow alley curved sharply down hill. To their right a grand looking temple with a faint glow of light somewhere behind typical massive pillars seemed to draw their attention. Behind them, the rhythmic - almost machine-like - pounding of leather sandals driven by powerful, well-trained legs was getting louder.

"In there," panted Max.

Lucius froze; he knew that building. There was something forbidden about it. It was a temple that was even more elitist than many of the most significant in Rome.

"Maximus, no," he said gravely.

"Lucius, this is no time to argue," Max insisted.

"But, Maximus, we can't," Lucius was pleading with Max now.

The sound of the ceaseless, running march of the soldiers was getting very loud indeed. They could now hear the clinking of metal too - sword against armour buckles. There was very little time. Chloe made the decision, calling to the others to follow her she ran to the temple and started to climb the steps towards the dim light.

Lucius was beside himself with what was happening; his usually calm expression was furrowed with worry. "But, the Vesta," he stammered, "The Temple of Vesta." He was the last one in the street and he had the dagger that his new-found friends seemed to need so much. There was very little choice; he would have to take his chance with the Vestals. Maybe they would be more forgiving than the pursuing soldiers. Lucius swallowed hard, took a deep breath then crossed the alley and disappeared into the dark recesses of the sacred Temple of Vesta - on pain of death.

Moments later, the soldiers arrived in the now deserted street. Standing on the same spot as the children had done split seconds ago, the platoon leader sniffed the air as he studied the possibilities.

"Hmmm," he pondered with lowered eyebrow, "They are in there." He was pointing to the temple.

"The Temple of Vesta, Captain Crassus?" asked a platoon member.

"Yes, soldier." Crassus grunted.

"But, that is a forbidden place, sir," continued the soldier.

"I know," said the platoon leader calmly.

"We can't interfere in-" the soldier was cut off as platoon leader Crassus whirled round and grasped him by the throat. He was determined to make his point almost lifting the questioning soldier off his feet. Eyebrow to eyebrows, he sneered down at his offending platoon member.

"I sincerely hope that you do not question my orders, Varo," he threatened, "Disobeying orders will lead to decimation, you understand."

"Not really, sir, no. I don't understand," choked Varo, "You can't decimate a platoon of four, sir."

"Can't I?" Crassus asked, more calmly, dropping a relieved Varo.

"No, sir. It's impossible to kill one in ten when there are only four, sir," Varo stated, very correctly and most definitely valiantly - few people crossed an angry Crassus.

"Then I will introduce a new punishment, Varo," Crassus grinned, "Quattuoration, Varo. Know what that is?"

"Quattuoration, sir?" Varo stammered.

"Yes, Varo. The killing of one in four," Crassus yelled, "And we won't bother drawing lots."

Varo stood down and saluted his submission. He had learned much about the short-fused Crassus; his Captain was right - even when he was wrong.

Crassus turned his attention back to the Temple of Vesta. "We will wait, platoon," he chuckled, "The Vestals may do our job for us and restore order by *removing any undesirables*. That will rid us of them. Children or not, Crassus will not stand by and see theft and anti-social behaviour from the youth of today menace the streets of Rome."

Chapter Eleven

Max's previous religious experiences had extended as far as a few weddings and the Christening of Chloe - he wasn't able to attend Kira's on account of him not actually existing at the time. The temple that they found themselves in was easily as grand as the churches and cathedrals of Christianity and shared many of the best intentions of those places of worship. The scale was vast and clearly designed to make mere mortals feel very small indeed. Unlike other Roman temples, The Temple of Vesta was circular and its pillars were laid out in rings. At the very heart was the inner sanctum and that was where the flickering glow that they had seen from the street was coming from.

Lucius appeared to be in some sort of shock. He was muttering something about needing protection and clearly was extremely agitated about being where he was.

Max coughed. "Don't reckon much to this incense," he spluttered.

Lucius broke his silence. "It is smoke," he said sullenly, scanning around for any signs of life, "From the sacred fire at the heart of the temple."

"I see," Max said, "Though if it gets any thicker, I won't be able to." He coughed some more to emphasise his witticism.

"Please, Maximus, you must not attract the attention of the Vestals," Lucius pleaded.

"Why, are they armed?" Max asked.

"No," Lucius answered.

"Then there must be lots of them," Max deduced.

"There are six."

"Then they must be really big blokes to worry you so much, Lucius," Max laughed.

"They are women."

"Women?" Max puzzled, "They don't have big dogs, do they?"

"Look!" cried Chloe, "There's a girl - a little girl."

There was. A little girl in white robes and headdress could be seen in the very heart of the temple. She was tending to a fire in an ornately carved open hearth - this was the sacred fire of Vesta. A fire that should not burn out until it was replenished on the 1st of March each year. Chloe's cry had startled the girl and she turned to see where the noise was coming from. On seeing the four intruders, she dropped the poker she was carrying and screamed - a full-bodied, high-pitched, ear-splitting scream. She was clearly quite unhappy.

"Now we are truly doomed," said Lucius, "She will bring the other Vestals and we will be killed."

"Killed?" questioned Kira.

"We have profaned the temple of the Goddess Vesta. The punishment is death. There are no exceptions - that is the sacred law," Lucius listed the facts of religious blasphemy in Ancient Rome solemnly.

"We should leave," Kira suggested - perhaps a little late.

"Sisters!" shrieked the girl tending the fire, "Sisters! Blasphemy! Profanity!"

"Blimey, she understands sisters really well," quipped Max, getting a sharp kick from Kira for his facetiousness.

Conscious of the need to attract no further attention, Kira approached the hysterical girl and tried to reassure her. "It's OK," she said, "We aren't here to harm you. We just need a little help."

The girl was hyper-ventilating, pointing wildly and repeating, "Unholy, unholy, unholy." She was pointing wildly at Max and Lucius her hand shaking furiously. Max was no expert on etiquette but he did know that this was, at the very least, quite rude.

"It's OK," repeated Kira, "We didn't mean to startle you. We mean you no harm."

"Unholy, unholy, polluted, unclean," she raved.

Max was mortified - he would have her know that he had recently started having two showers a week and was even experimenting with the use of a deodorant body spray (a disappointing Christmas gift given by a distant Great Aunt).

"I am Kira," she continued, "What is your name? Please, we really won't harm you."

The girl steadied a little and took a deep breath. "Concordia," she revealed, her facial features un-knitting and the redness fading from a less angry demeanour.

"That's better," Kira continued her supportive role, "Nice to meet you, Concordia. This is Chloe and this is Lucius and Max - imus."

At the mention of the boys, Concordia went wild again - pulling her robes tight as if to keep out germs then prostrating herself in front of the hearth and begging forgiveness for allowing the contamination of her temple.

"Steady on, Concordia, that's a little harsh," said Max.

"You do not understand, Maximus, men are not allowed to enter here. Not ever. If men are discovered in the Temple of Vesta, they are always put to death and any Vestal found guilty of letting them enter would be sentenced to being buried alive," Lucius issued another grave statement.

"Men? You said men. What about boys? Does that rule apply to boys? Is there a cut off point? A safe age? An age, which I will definitely be much younger than, to avoid death?" Max was desperate but knew deep down that it was just being male that was the problem with this particular profanity.

Kira had crossed to the hearth and was trying to console

Concordia once more. She now knew from what Lucius had said that Concordia feared for her own life as she would be held responsible for allowing these unholy intruders and could also pay the ultimate penalty.

"Concordia. Concordia, please listen to me," Kira was now pleading. "I know this must be very frightening for you but I really want you to know that we don't want to get you into any trouble."

"It is too late. The blasphemy has taken place and I am to blame," she sobbed, tears pouring from pale blue eyes.

Chloe had crossed to join Kira. She sat, cross-legged next to the distraught Vestal and fiddled uncomfortably with her trainers-doing her best to understand.

"We need your help, Concordia. We need help to escape from here. We need to get back to our own - land," Kira explained as best she could.

"We are all on a journey, sister," sobbed Concordia.

"Very deep," spluttered Max facetiously, receiving glares from just about everyone.

"Concordia, if you help us, no-one needs to know that we were even here. We will be safe - and so will you," Kira made a good case for everyone's continued survival.

Concordia had at last begun to listen properly and Kira was able to explain further. Confining her story to the reclaiming of the dagger, which was of course rightfully theirs, Kira revealed how they had sought refuge from the soldiers who wanted to take it from them and punish them for the *theft* of their own property. Concordia, calm now, listened carefully.

Outside, Crassus did his best to be patient, but the frustration of being prevented from reaching justice was difficult for him to understand. For Crassus, a soldier should not just uphold the law but a soldier should *be* the law and administer justice swiftly and effectively. Being mere metres from his goal yet being prevented from acting by the gods was simply unacceptable for a man of honour and action. He had an idea. The House of the Vestals stood next to the temple itself and if the priestesses of Vesta were not worshipping in the temple, they would be there. Crassus may not be allowed to enter The Temple of Vesta but there was no such prevention for entering the Vestal House.

"Platoon - move out!" he ordered, his top lip curled in utter contempt for having to wait for any time at all. The soldiers quickly rallied to his call and within moments were marching in military precision to the Vestal House that adjoined the temple. Statues of the Vestals in their priestess robes stood in alcoves either side of the main door on which Crassus was now thumping with a massive sledge-hammer fist. "Sisters of Vesta," Crassus yelled, shattering the peace of the Roman night. "Mighty Sisters, there has been an intrusion. A band of highly dangerous criminals is hiding in the Temple of Vesta. In the very inner sanctum of the flame," he lied.

There were sounds of movement behind the door. Heavy bolts were pushed back - many heavy bolts. The heavy oak door eased open enough to reveal a cowled figure in the shadows within.

"What do you know of the inner sanctum of the flame, soldier?" the figure asked.

"Only what I have been told," answered Crassus.

The figure stepped from the shadows of the Vestal House and into the moonlight of the street. She lowered her hood and Crassus recognised her immediately. Out of respect for her position as Maxima Vestalis - the highest priestess of Vesta - Crassus placed himself on one knee in front of her. The platoon, following his example, took a few steps back and did the same - their heads bowed.

"Maxima Vestalis, Aquillia," Crassus addressed the woman, "Your temple has been profaned and I offer my services in achieving justice for you and the Vestals."

"Do you indeed, Captain?" she smiled, knowing exactly what this power hungry soldier was after. Aquillia replaced her hood and obscured her sharp features once more, completely hiding her identity. She slowly walked down the house steps and gently swept past Crassus in the direction of her temple. When she had passed, Crassus stood up and watched her gliding movement. In many ways, she was very much like him - he thought. Just like him, she had given over thirty years of her life to something she believed in absolutely. Snapping free from his daydream, Crassus coughed to alert his platoon that they should prepare for action. They stood to attention and he smiled. He had them now.

Deep within The Temple of Vesta, Concordia had done her best to listen to the strangers. "I understand, Kira, but I am a mere novice and have no influence with the High Priestess Aquillia. If she were to find you here, we would all surely perish," she explained.

"We don't need to ask her, Concordia, we just need a safe getaway. Is there another exit? Some kind of back door or even a secret passageway?" Kira was in her element now, organising a great escape.

"There is only a servants' route to The Vestal House," Concordia revealed, "It is used by the lower priestesses like me for tending the fire and other temple duties."

"Sounds absolutely perfect," enthused Kira.

"How so?" asked Max. "I take it that's where the man-hating Vestals live? Wouldn't that be like going into the lion's den?"

"You're obsessed with lions, Max," Kira pointed out.

"And big dogs," added Chloe.

"You know what I mean," he went on irritatedly, "There will be five more Vestals in there."

"And there may be a means of disguise in there!" Kira smiled. She clearly had a plan.

Max waited for the clever spectacles to appear but there was no time. Further planning was interrupted by a voice coming from the temple entrance. It was Aquilla, making an offering prayer to Vesta before entering the sacred depths of the inner sanctum.

"Quickly," urged Concordia, fearing for all their lives, "Behind the sanctum wall is a small opening. The passage is dark and narrow. Feel your way along using the walls and stop when you come to the steps with your feet. I will speak to Maxima Vestalis Aquillia. Quickly! Go now!" Concordia gestured for them to go. To be discovered was certain death. Kira, Chloe, Max and Lucius left the inner sanctum in search of the passageway to safety.

Just as the children left, Aquilla entered. Her hood lowered in respect to the goddess and she prostrated herself before the flame. Concordia followed her example and for a moment there was silence in worship.

"Novice Concordia?" said Aquillia, gently. She stood and Concordia could see the stern expression on her very serious face. It was as though the Maxima Vestalis would be able to spot deceit just by looking at her.

Concordia looked up and into Aquillia's deep gaze and reluctantly made eye contact with those focused grey eyes. Aquillia smiled and her face softened - after all, thirty years ago, she had been the novice and knew how difficult it was to meet the demands of the rules of the House of Vesta.

"Yes, Maxima Vestalis?" Concordia answered, reverently.

Aquillia's gentle but persuasive tone continued, "Concordia, it is two years since you were selected from the house of Caesar to achieve the greatest honour as a Vestal, isn't it?"

"Yes, Maxima Vestalis. It was my Uncle Julius who recommended me."

"Yes, that's right, it was," Aquillia chuckled at the irony that Julius Caesar would probably very soon declare himself Emperor and therefore automatically become Pontifex Maximus - the High

Priest overseeing the Vestals and, therefore, the only man permitted to enter the sacred Temple of Vesta. "I understand that this life is very difficult to follow. To give up so much is a great responsibility for a young mind," Aquillia suddenly became more intense, her sharp features seemed more accentuated by the flickering light from the flames as her expression hardened again. "It would be understandable if certain rules were broken," she paused, "If - perhaps accidentally - a novice were to let strangers into the temple, maybe."

Concordia swallowed hard - she was responsible for profaning the temple and now she must lie to the Maxima Vestalis for what she thought was a righteous cause, "I have done nothing but perform my honest duty to the goddess, Maxima Vestalis."

Aquillia paused again. "I see," she said finally, "The goddess Vesta can ask nothing more than that." She glanced over at the flames. "The fire seems a little low. Perhaps you will need to go to the Vestal House for - more wood?"

In that moment, Concordia knew that Aquillia had guessed correctly what she was up to and judged it to be acceptable. Even Vesta could accept a few broken rules it seemed. Concordia bowed and hurried to the passageway. Aquillia gave a quick dedication to the flames and drifted calmly away and back to the street outside.

The passageway was pitch black. Max tried not to think about it but when you can't see anything at all, it is difficult to spot a distraction. Reaching out to the walls, he caught his hand on something sharp, "Ouch," he yelped.

"Sorry, Maximus," came Lucius' disembodied voice.

Max had put his hand on the dagger that Lucius was still - thankfully - carrying.

"Listen," whispered Kira, "Someone is coming."

Indeed they were. A small temple lamp was bouncing its way

down the passage towards them - carried by a much relieved Concordia.

"Concordia, are we glad to see you," Max breathed - more pleased to have a bit of light than another girl in his party.

"I have seen the High Priestess Aquillia," Concordia began, "I think she suspects something."

"Great - roll out the lions," added Max.

Concordia ignored him. Lots of people did that, Max thought. "She will do nothing to stop you getting home," she added, "But we must be quick. Kira, take this lamp and carry on to the House door. When you reach it, push gently as it scrapes and could wake the Sisters. We will gather on the other side of the door and I will show you what to do next."

The lamp was passed down the line. "Couldn't I carry the light?" asked Max when he got his hands on it.

"Scaredy cat," jibed Chloe, and the lamp moved on to Kira.

In front of her were about ten stone steps then a short section of passageway to the serving door of the House of Vesta. Kira climbed and moved quickly to the end of the passageway with the aid of the lamp. Max tripped up six of the stairs, scraped his elbow on the passageway wall and got a sharp poke in the back from the dagger when he ran into Chloe and then Lucius ran into him. He snatched it from Lucius to avoid further injury. Kira gently opened the heavy door with the minimum of noise and everyone went through.

Gathered on the other side of the door - within the House of Vesta - they all looked around. Astonishingly, it looked to Max like they were in the Vestal Laundry.

Aquillia appeared at the entrance to the temple, drifting ghost-like from the shadows. Crassus bowed in reverence once more, slyly looking for the intruders that he was sure she must have found.

"I'm afraid that you have had an unnecessary wait, Captain," she smiled, "Your reprobates must be long gone. There is no evidence of any profanity in my temple."

Crassus' eyebrow lowered even more until it connected with his Roman nose. He jumped upright and leapt towards the steps of the temple. He absolutely would find the disruptive elements.

"TIBERIUS PARSIMONIUS CRASSUS!" she shrieked, "Step one foot on the sacred ground of the Temple of Vesta and your life will be over."

Crassus froze - partly from the threat to his life but mostly through the amazement that she knew his full name. He took a step back and watched as Aquillia floated back to the House of Vesta.

"Magnificent!" he announced, in total awe of the Maxima Vestalis. It was at that moment that he became aware of the sniggering from his platoon. He whirled round to confront the insubordination. "Mention my middle name to anyone," he threatened, "And it won't be decimation or quattuoration - it will be unusation!"

"The killing of one in one, sir?" asked Varo.

"Absolutely, Trooper Varo, absolutely."

The sniggering stopped.

Maxima Vestalis Aquillia was standing in the door way of The House of Vesta blessing her fellow Sisters as they left for what must be some sort of late night ceremony. She blessed all four of them as they came down the house steps robed and hooded.

"Peace and harmony be with you on your holy voyage, Sisters," she called.

The group of Sisters were an interesting sight. Shorter than Aquillia, especially the second one - Crassus assumed that they must be young novices.

"Sisters," he bowed as they passed.

"Unholy masculine types," greeted the leading Vestal.

"An honour," Crassus blushed in total ignorance.

"Vesta go with you," called Concordia who had appeared at Aquillia's side.

"And also with you, sister," replied the rather too high-pitched third Sister - waving her dagger in farewell.

Crassus watched them go. Such devotion to duty at this late hour - marvellous. They rounded the corner past the temple and were gone. Wait a minute - a Vestal with a blade? Crassus had realised too late.

"What? A blade? A Vestal with a knife! Wait - it's a disguise - they are the disruptive elements! Platoon - pursue!" he bawled.

A little less militarily precise, the platoon gathered their wits and ran after the imposter Vestals. Aquillia smiled - Vestal victory over machismo disappointment.

Chapter Twelve

When things don't quite make sense, the mind seems to go into a higher gear. Max was now discarding his borrowed Vestal robes and giggling with his sisters and Lucius about the absurdity of their situation. They had just managed to get past a supposedly highly trained centurion, disguised as Vestal Priestesses. That was a thought that he never ever expected to have until today - that thought along with several hundred other thoughts and ideas that could only be considered as part of the day's nonsensical, illogical and, very probably, impossible events. Yet, Max still had not woken up - so if this was a dream, it was a very graphic and long one.

Suddenly though, any further thoughts were shelved as they all realised that the Roman soldiers had seen through their plan a little quicker than they had anticipated. The platoon appeared at the very edge of the Forum where the children now stood- just three hundred metres away.

"Where now?" panicked Chloe.

"The Market Place," answered Kira, "Where it all started."

"This way," shouted Lucius as he sped off with the advantage of being a native.

The Market Place was a short run from the Forum. Empty now, it was very different from the bustling centre it had been earlier today.

"Now what? Is a door just going to appear?" Max had real doubts about Kira's theory.

"I don't know, Max," so did she - it seemed, "The whole time-travel thing is a bit new to me."

"Well, over there is where we arrived," Max pointed to the spot where they had all hidden behind Mr. Sabre's cart of amphora. It seemed such a long time ago.

There was a shout in the distance - sadly, though, not distant enough from them. It was Crassus, "They've cut through to the Market Place! Platoon- very quick march!"

Chloe began to cry. It had all been too much and she was extremely tired. "What about, Lucius? What's going to happen to him if we get away?" she sobbed.

Lucius grabbed Chloe around the shoulders and squeezed her tightly in reassurance, "I will be fine. My Master is very fair with his punishment," he explained.

"Punishment?" squeaked Chloe, upset again.

"I am a slave. I ran away - so, I will be punished. Just go, friends, all will be well."

Crassus' platoon thundered into the Market Place, helmeted, shield-bearing and leather armour clad, they skidded to a halt.

"There they are! Seize the public menaces! Use force - even if totally unnecessary," Crassus snarled as the platoon marched ominously closer.

Max took Lucius by the hand and gripped it tightly. He shook it in what was a very mature manner. "Thanks, Lucius," he said.

Kira was searching for a miracle; willing an exit to the future to appear in the shape of a totally anachronistic Tudor oak door. The exact spot had to be around here somewhere. She remembered *that* particular fountain and water trough from this morning. *That* pillared walkway was familiar too.

Then, there it was.

Really, it was.

On the edge of a Roman market place in 44 B.C. stood a solid oak Tudor door. It was slightly ajar and a warm light from the future was spilling through into the Roman night, giving the oak panelling a cosy, inviting glow and highlighting the paint of the 'No Entry' sign. Kira was right - and what was more, Max could feel it now, the dagger in his hand buzzed and tingled like it was infused with static electricity. It was definitely the key to their door to the future - to their *present* lives.

The group farewell to the genuine Roman slave called Lucius came to an end as Crassus and his men charged across the square towards them.

"It is really there," Kira was struggling to comprehend her own theory, "We can get home."

Kira and Chloe ran the last few metres to the door then stopped. What was Max doing?

"Come with us," Max was saying to Lucius - most definitely without thinking.

"Max! We have to go!" yelled Chloe.

"I know," shouted Max waving the dagger in exasperation. This was probably going to be one of those moments when good choices, decisions or moves are completely ignored - again. Max grabbed Lucius by the hand and dragged him towards the Tudor doorway to *their* present. To a future for Lucius that he couldn't possible imagine - let alone comprehend.

"Where are we going?" Lucius pulled back and stopped Max in his tracks.

"To safety, Lucius. I promise."

"Max, Quick!" Kira was insistent.

She was just fifteen metres ahead of him and he was thirty metres in front of the rapidly advancing soldiers. "Is it our time? Our place?" Max asked.

Chloe peered through the gap, tentatively. "There's people. In proper clothes. There's that boring tour person," she paused as her heart skipped with joy, "Mum and Dad - there's Mum and Dad."

"Come on then," pleaded Kira. The soldiers were twenty metres away with murderous intent.

"Come with us, Lucius," Max was desperate now - desperate to save the slave from any punishment, "Come with us and we will bring you back later."

"Move away from that door and you will not be harmed!" yelled Crassus - fifteen metres away, "Much!"

Chloe's little face turned to Max and she slipped through the door. It was the happiest that Max had ever seen her. Kira looked back at her brother - he was pushing Lucius towards the door with his left hand and swinging the dagger back towards the furious Crassus. "Kira, take Lucius," he pleaded and Kira grabbed Lucius by his wrist.

"Maximus!" called Lucius as he was bundled through the door - disappearing into a world he would never understand. Kira had spun round standing between two different times.

"Max, come on!" she called to him, tears streaming down her face.

"No you don't! Stop right there!"

It was Crassus - Captain Tiberius Parsimonius Crassus of the fifteenth legion - who reached out for Max. His huge and sweaty palms slid down Max's arm towards his hand. Kira's face was filled with horror as she stepped backwards two thousand and sixty-five years into the future - and was gone. Crassus' big grasp tore at the dagger that killed Julius Caesar and wrenched it from Max's grip - breaking the link.

Max looked to the doorway - the Tudor doorway - from Rome in 44 B.C. to London in 2021 A.D. He stared as the door winked out of existence and his real time and place in the world vanished for good.

Chapter Thirteen

Kira was nearly three when Max was born. Mum would still tell people the story that, when she first saw him in the hospital, Kira had asked why he was so expensive - at seven pounds, thirteen. Usually, Kira would smile at this re-telling. Not now. Not today. Eleven years on and she had lost her brother. After having to deliver some very complicated explanations, things were going to be very different. Who would she be able to shout at if other things were frustrating her? How could she possibly accept that she had actually lost something herself? It had been so easy just to blame Max.

She wiped the tears from her cheeks and tried to blot out the final image of her brother - a little boy just trying to get home; desperately reaching for the impossible doorway that would bring him back to what he knew; the harrowing look of disappointment as that thug, Crassus, ripped the dagger from him and condemned him to - well, to who knew what? Kira dragged her thoughts back to the present; as well as numb from the events she had just been part of, she could feel a marked difference in temperature. Swapping the warmth of the Mediterranean for the cool brightness of British October sun merely drew more attention to their return and what they had left behind and what they had brought with them.

Chloe tugged Kira's sleeve. "Max," she muttered but Kira could say nothing. They had always been indestructible - making sometimes clever, sometimes lucky escapes from their escapades - but this adventure was too big. Spanning miles, centuries and cultures. It had defeated them.

Max William Foster really was ancient history.

Lucius too was silent. There had been no time to explain what might happen if he had entered that door in the Market Place. At best, he had expected a hiding place until the soldiers had given up - somewhere to plan how he would explain his actions to his master. At worst, he had expected finding himself in another forbidden inner sanctum and receiving punishment for blasphemy. This was neither of those possibilities and defied Roman explanation. The doorway they were standing in was now connecting two rooms. In front - a corridor full of people in the similar strange clothing of his new friends; and behind - a dusty room crammed with many collected objects. The Market Place was not there. Rome was not there. There was a lady at the front of the crowd who spoke of trees but not in a way that he could truly understand.

"Fascinatingly, oak trees can live for over one thousand years. Oak has medullary ray cells, which radiate from the centre of the log like the curved spokes of a wheel! The rift, or comb grain effect, is obtained by cutting at an angle of about fifteen degrees off the quartered position," she was rubbing the dark walls reverently. So this was indeed a temple - a temple to the goddess Oak.

Kira let go of the door to the Cabinet of Curiosities and it swung shut a little too hard, leaving them stranded at the back of the tour in the corridor. The Tour Guide stopped and stared, her facial expression of total disgust visible from twenty metres. "The wood! Respect the wood!" she spat - then realising that this may have come across as a little harsh, she added, "Please." Though she had much bigger worries, Kira found herself saying sorry.

Satisfied with an apology the Tour Guide continued and Kira stopped listening. Her mind was racing - full of ideas and schemes. She needed some time to think. She needed some air. She wasn't going to get either though as among the people who had turned to stare at her, whilst she was being berated for mistreating a door, were Mum and Dad. Smiling, they were politely excusing themselves and working their way back through the tour party to Kira, Chloe and - Lucius. There was no time to think.

"Mum and Dad," gasped Chloe, excited but also realising that explaining this was going to be impossible.

"Alright, kids?" Dad said, jovially.

"Great, Dad," Kira lied.

"Fascinating, isn't it?" he went on, "History, I mean, it is fascinating." He had no idea of the dramatic irony in that statement. Then, it came - the question that Kira and Chloe couldn't answer with any certainty or credibility.

"Oh, where's Max?" asked Mum.

Kira and Chloe were as quick as they possibly could be with their lies and simultaneously answered.

"Gift shop," rushed Kira.

"Toilet," hurried Chloe.

"Gift - shop - toilet," covered Kira, "Gift shop toilet."

Mum and Dad smiled - happy with that explanation. "Who's your friend?" asked Mum.

"Lucius, Mum," answered Chloe, without thinking.

She needn't have worried though - oblivious to his tunic, leather sandals and rough-hewn copper bracelet that were all totally anachronistic and unsuitable for an Autumn day in the United Kingdom - Dad merely said, "What a charming, old-fashioned name."

Lucius bowed and said, "Thank you, sir." but again, no ancient etiquette alarm bells rang and Mrs. Foster just said how nice it was to see young men with manners.

"Hmmm," pondered Dad, "Knew a Marcus in school -" However, before he could re-live that particular tale, they were all aware of the irritated coughing of the Tour Guide. She wanted to move on. Dad patted Kira patronisingly, tussled Chloe's hair and nodded to Lucius. Mum blew them all a kiss and they both returned to their place as suckers for punishment on the front row.

"If you would like to follow me, ladies and gentlemen, we will now go and look at a wonderful, curving, oak Tudor staircase.

Look out for the carved animal heads; one of which represents a tale from Aesop!" informed the Tour Guide - again.

This was like *Ground Hog Day* - only not funny. Kira realised that they had arrived back here from Rome just before they left - a further impossibility that meant that their day in Ancient Rome had taken *negative time*. The tour party moved forward, leaving Kira, Chloe and Lucius in the corridor - each stunned for a different reason.

"We've got the rubbishest parents ever," Chloe voiced what Kira was thinking, "They didn't notice Lucius is a Roman and they believed all that bunk about gift shop toilets. They are really rubbish."

Kira smiled at the fact that Chloe's vocabulary contained the word 'bunk'.

"Where is this temple?" asked Lucius.

"Oh," said Kira bracing herself for a difficult explanatory time ahead, "This isn't a temple, Lucius."

"It is like nothing I have seen in Rome," he went on.

"That's absolutely right," agreed Kira.

"If the Market Place is through there," Lucius pointed to the closed door of the Cabinet of Curiosities, "On the other side of the room of trinkets, then we should wait until the coast is clear and I will return to Brutus and explain everything."

Kira would have loved to see him try. "The Market Place isn't through there," she said, "In fact, I very much doubt that Rome is."

Lucius did not understand. He may have gone through a door, perhaps even two doors, but if he could enter a building then he could exit it in the same way. "Through here," he said as he opened the Cabinet of Curiosities and stepped inside. Kira and Chloe followed.

Familiar to the girls, the organised clutter lay as they had first found it - including Chloe's little cardigan, discarded during happier times but now gratefully retrieved and put on again. Chloe too was feeling the eerie coolness of their current situation. Unfamiliar to Lucius, he strode to the three other doors in the room. He opened each dark door in turn - revealing absolutely nothing but further oak-panelled corridors. "Where am I?" he puzzled.

"Start with *when am I?*" said Kira.

"When?"

"You've heard of Britain? Of Britannia?" Kira offered.

"Of course. My master was part of Caesar's campaign of conquest there."

"Well," Kira braced herself for the reaction, "You're there. In Britannia."

"Impossible," Lucius could not accept this, "The distance - it is many leagues from Rome. Many days travel."

"Try -" Kira was on a roll and could see no point in telling anything but the truth, "Two thousand years. Or there abouts." Lucius was completely stumped. "I'm sorry, Lucius, we don't really understand either. All *I* know is that Max is trapped a long way away - and ago. And you? You most definitely shouldn't be here. Not now. Not here."

There was another voice in the room - an older one, "Children may have many fine qualities but it appears that *listening* is not one of them."

"Jupiter!" cried Lucius, throwing himself to the floor in reverence to *the father of the gods*.

"An Ancient Roman," said Sir Walter Cope darkly, closing the third oak door behind him and entering the room. "The finest example I have seen this side of the crucifixion," Sir Walter paused and pushed his flowing white hair back from his forehead. "What have you done?"

"We can explain," started Chloe as she finished concentrating on multi-coloured cardigan buttons.

"No we can't," Kira snapped.

"I do not need explanations," said Sir Walter, quite severely now, "I made a request of you all. I asked you to take nothing and bring nothing back. And you have done both."

"It was a bit more cryptic than that!" said Kira, angrily.

"You are an intelligent young lady - but clearly not intelligent enough to heed my warning and certainly not intelligent enough to think of the consequences of your actions." Sir Walter was glowering at the children now. He strode to Lucius and bent down to get him to his feet. In doing so, his deep blue eyes met Lucius' confused gaze. "You have visited Ancient Rome. The dagger that killed Julius Caesar is missing. It must have taken you there." He paused and took a calming breath, steadying himself for an answer he already knew, "Where is it now?"

"It is with Maximus, my Lord," Lucius stammered, still believing he was in the company of a god.

"Maximus?"

"Max - our brother," said Chloe, heavily. Looking down sadly, she realised her buttons were done up wrong. At six, this was all too much. Tired and worried she tore her cardigan open and crossly started buttoning again as a tear broke from sad eyes to roll down her cheek.

"And, where is - Max?" asked Sir Walter, somewhat coldly.

"In the market place by the Forum, my Lord," answered Lucius, bowing with misplaced respect.

"The Forum in Ancient Rome," Sir Walter mused, "This is very serious."

That was a statement that everyone present understood. Kira, Chloe and now Lucius all looked to Sir Walter Cope - Knight of Queen Elizabeth's College of Antiquaries and current holder of more secrets than he cared to share. Abruptly, he spat, "Max is trapped. He must live his life in Ancient Rome and Lucius must live his life here. There is no other way. It is a fair exchange."

Sir Walter's announcement hit them hard. "Exchange? No!" yelled Kira.

"There is no alternative, child. The dagger is the only Ancient Roman item in the collection - though it was originally discovered quite by chance, many leagues from Rome."

Sir Walter was becoming distant as he recalled the events from his long memory.

"Where?" urged Kira.

"Oh, it's not significant. Not important," Sir Walter looked weary - even older than before.

"Where, Mr. Cope, please." Kira seemed to be on to something.

"Why, in this very city. In London," he revealed.

"Exactly where, Mr. Cope? I think it may be very significant indeed." Kira was extremely animated. Could it be that she saw a glimmer of hope in finding Max?

"Why, in the *Globe Theatre*."

"Shakespeare's Globe? On the South Bank?" Kira asked.

"In Southwark, yes." Sir Walter's answer seemed to knock the wind from Kira's sails.

"Then it was found recently. Shakespeare's Globe is new. A modern reconstruction," Kira's voice fell flat as her fledgling theory seemed to collapse.

"In the *original* Globe, child," added Sir Walter.

"Original?" asked Chloe - who like Lucius was lost in this conversation after her distraction by little cardigan buttons.

Kira clarified the situation a little with what she knew, "*The Globe Theatre* on the south bank of the River Thames is actually a very modern building - built to the best *guesstimates* of experts on Shakespeare. The real *Globe Theatre* was just down the road, I think - set back a little further from the Thames." Kira was smiling inside as she made use of her knowledge and experience once more. She was very glad that *standing* in the yard of the New *Globe Theatre* to watch three and a half hours of *The Merchant of Venice* had been worth the confusion and back ache.

"Yes, child, but how does this have any significance?" snapped Sir Walter, impatiently. He was keen to understand why Kira was suddenly so excited after being so distraught about her brother's fate.

"One more detail, please, Mr. Cope. *When* was it found?"

Sir Walter was beginning to see what she was getting at. She was trying to construct a pathway using the objects in the room as stepping stones through time "It somehow ended up as a prop in the very first performance of *Julius Caesar* on the -" Sir Walter was thinking hard - it was important to help to repair the situation the children had accidentally created, "The 12th of June, 1599."

Aware of the irony of the place and event but more concerned with the date, Kira was elated, "An exact date! That is an exact date. I take it as the dagger was responsible for our accidental visit to Rome, we just need an item to get us to -"

A wry smile broke on Sir Walter's ancient face. He was ahead of her and cut her off, " - to 1599. The dagger was collected with the very quill used to write the very script of the play of -"

"Julius Caesar!" Kira smiled as the irony ramped up.

Chloe found it. Rushing to the table at which Max had been standing, she held it aloft and cried with great excitement, "Shakespeare's quill!" Then she thought for a bit and her elation vanished, "No, still don't understand." She looked to Lucius, "And Lucius is really lost."

"It is simple," beamed Kira. Then, looking at the confusion from the other two children, she offered her explanation, "I'm going to get, Max. Remember what I said about the dagger *taking* us to Rome?" Chloe nodded. Sir Walter marvelled at her skills of deduction; at how she was weaving a patch from new possibilities to cover the gaping hole in historical events created by their clumsy Roman expedition. Lucius stared blankly. Kira continued, "Well, if I am right, every object in this Cabinet of Curiosities can do that and potentially, we can go anywhere that the objects came from - I mean *anywhen*, I suppose! What I should say is that we can visit any time that these objects came from. Any time they were first used. If we use the quill, we can get the dagger." Though all of this was a stretch of even the most fertile imagination, Kira was actually - of course - absolutely right. Sir Walter had said that the dagger and the quill were collected together so one could possibly be used to go back and find the other.

"1599 is not Ancient Rome, child, you must work harder," Sir Walter was enjoying this. Had Kira not been caught up in the excitement of her realisation, she may have found his reaction to all this a little creepy.

"I'm getting there," she said, merely a little annoyed at his doubts about her plan, "We would need to bring the dagger here to the Cabinet of Curiosities. Put back the quill then leave through one of the doors just carrying the dagger."

"Which will take you to where it originally came from!" Sir Walter applauded, as if somehow relieved.

"Ancient Rome!" laughed Kira.

"Max!" Chloe smiled.

"I am afraid I do not understand your words, Kira," said Lucius, sadly.

"Oh, Lucius, it doesn't matter because we *can* get you home and we can get Max back," Kira rubbed Lucius' shoulder as she tried to reassure him. He merely needed to trust her.

"What you propose, child, is - possible," said Sir Walter slowly. Kira sensed another warning. "But you must only do what is necessary. Find the dagger and bring it back here again. Whatever you do, do not lose the quill." There was a long pause as everyone tried to understand the facts and complexities of what was to be done. Sir Walter broke the silence again, "Perhaps I should go and take charge of the situation. I should go back to 1599."

"Back?" asked Kira, "You've been before?"

"Yes. Yes I have," he said, thoughtfully.

"No, Sir Walter," Kira protested, "This is our -"

"Adventure!" chipped in Chloe.

"I was going to say problem," Kira added.

"Either word holds great danger, children," warned Sir Walter as he turned to Lucius, "And for you, young Roman, this is beyond all reasoning. I know just how it feels. 1599 was where it all started - for me also."

Chapter Fourteen

"Next!" he boomed and the small boy crumbled in front of him. Shoulders dropped and head low, the rejected lad climbed from the magnificently decorated stage into the straw covered yard and out into a muddy Elizabethan obscurity.

The greatest writer in the English language wasn't having a good year. It was slightly improved on 1598 - a year which had ended with the all time low of his acting company, *The Lord Chamberlain's Men*, stealing a theatre for Christmas. Perhaps stealing was too dramatic a word and it was certainly no Christmas gift. In truth, they owned the building outright but had had landlord problems over the site it stood on - so on the 28th of December, instead of Christmas revelries with his wife and daughters in Stratford-upon-Avon, he had been standing with mallet in hand in a very frozen east London. The landlord, Mr. Giles Allen, was out of town for Christmas and when he returned, his land was empty. Actors and the playwright alike had dismantled *The Theatre* and carried it beam by beam to their carpenter's yard and, eventually, when the weather improved, to Southwark where it would be resurrected as *The Globe*.

That is where the problems really started. The land they had bought for *The Globe* turned out to be a marsh and was extremely susceptible to flooding. Months of valuable time had been lost on the construction of an artificial island for the new playhouse just to take it above the level of any possible tidal surge. Construction was, what the impossibly optimistic carpenter Peter Street described as - 'ongoing'. 'Ongoing' seemed to mean going on and on - and on. It was certainly 'ongoing' right now with the thuds of mallet on chisel and the rhythmic tearing of handsaws.

Amongst all this activity, no-one had noticed the arrival of a finely crafted oak door signed 'No Entry' - excepting the fact that it winked into existence in the middle of the theatre yard, it blended in perfectly with the period. Amongst all this noise, no-one could hear the harsh tearing of two realities in collision. With much commotion, yet totally disregarded, 2021 crashed into 1599 and left three shaken youngsters in its wake.

"Will we never find a replacement? 'Twas most inconsiderate of young Thomas to come down with a sickness," came a voice from the shadows of the lower seats.

"'*Twas* plague, Will," answered a proud looking man on the centre of the pillared stage.

"I know, Burbage - but the play is tomorrow! *Julius Caesar* opens tomorrow!" frantic, he stood up and leaned over the lower balustrade.

"Now, Will," said the man on the stage, "'Tis possible to get too attached to your work and over react." He adjusted his burgundy doublet and strode confidently to the very edge of the rostra.

"Master Burbage, need I remind you how much depends on this opening performance, even if it is an unworthy scribbling by such a lowly hack as yours truly. A good return is essential - or *The Lord Chamberlain's Men* will tread the path that they will never return!" the frantic man tugged at his dark goatee beard, huffing loudly.

"So dramatic, Master Shakespeare!" said Burbage as he came down from the stage and looked up at William Shakespeare. "If it is profit you want, you should be doing one of Marlowe's plays. They always bring in a goodly crowd."

Shakespeare was inconsolable, striding from the lower gallery to face the taller Burbage, "Christopher Marlowe has not written a word for five years - on account of him being very dead - and yet still his name is remembered. People cannot even spell mine!"

"Perhaps spelling it the same way once or twice yourself would help, Will," laughed Burbage.

"I am creative," announced Shakespeare pompously, "I experiment with words."

"True, Will, true - but it would help you publish if you just stopped experimenting with your surname," Burbage was laughing a big hearty laugh as he clapped William Shakespeare between his shoulder blades. Will was glad he had chosen not to wear his ruff today for he would have surely choked from a blow like that.

Still exposed in the theatre yard, Kira, Chloe and Max's Roman replacement, Lucius, had almost recovered from their disorientating arrival and were taking in their new, very different and wonderous surroundings. Chloe had insisted on carrying the quill - a bit like how she insisted on pressing every lift and traffic crossing button she came across - but now Kira thought it best to remove it from her to keep it safe. Chloe had lost many things over her six years and even now, discarded dummies from three or four years ago were being discovered in shoe boxes, book cases and stuffed into Mum's ornaments and vases.

"That's him," whispered Chloe as she reluctantly gave up the quill.

"Shakespeare, yes. Incredible," said Kira, "He's not as ugly as his portrait." Kira was thinking of one of the few famous images of him - the one that made it look like he had been decapitated and his head presented on a plate, big eyes bulging fish-like from the humiliation of having no body. He certainly had more hair than his portrait and even though his hairline was receding, his dark, wavy, shoulder-length hair could almost have given him membership of one of Dad's mystical bands from '*the* noughties'.

Another small Elizabethan urchin had climbed the stage to present his talents to Shakespeare.

"Mr Shackaspee?" said the boy.

"Shakespeare," groaned Will.

"'Tis not what is written here," argued the boy looking at a small piece of manuscript he was holding. Shakespeare marched to the stage and climbed the wooden steps to stand towering over the boy. He grabbed the manuscript, perused it for a moment with eyebrows knotted and realised the boy had a point.

"NEXT!" he yelled in response then composed himself and turned to Burbage. "Alas, your Brutus still needs a servant, Burbage."

Richard Burbage, self-styled finest actor of his age, strutted up the steps and flounced towards Shakespeare. He stuck out his broad chest, threw back his head and overacted his lines as Brutus from Shakespeare's newest play. "What, Lucius, ho! When, Lucius, when?" he bellowed.

It was automatic; written into the very fibre of his being - Lucius could simply not help it as he ran forward and said with true Roman gusto, "Called you, My Lord?"

Burbage stopped his wild gesticulating and he and Will exchanged joyous smiles - unaware of the other rejected lad glancing sadly back for a possible reconsideration as he meandered his way through the theatre yard.

"Hey, nonny, nonny!" called Burbage, "A natural, Will. He is a natural!"

"And, he knows the words - *my* words!" spluttered Shakespeare.

"Thou art clearly more famous than I would have thee realise, Will," laughed Burbage, loudly.

William Shakespeare took a step towards the new arrivals, looking down only at Lucius for a part in his new play. Lucius could indeed play 'Lucius'. The dramatic irony was ramping up some more.

"What are you called, boy?" Shakespeare asked.

"Lucius, sir," was the honest reply.

"What a confident rascal!" said Burbage, striding to Will's side.

"He is of the right age," mused Shakespeare.

"His clothing leaves a little to be desired," grunted Burbage, "Not very - Roman."

"Yet he has a goodly look about him," insisted Shakespeare.

Burbage and Will turned to each other, shook hands heartily and both said together, "He'll do!"

"What will he do, Mister Shakespeare?" asked Kira.

It was the first time that Shakespeare and Burbage had really paid any attention to the other two young people in the yard and when they did it was as if they had learned that hell was empty and a couple of the devils were here in the theatre having taken the malevolent form of -

"Women!" Shakespeare spluttered.

"They are women, Will!" Burbage agreed, struck down with the self same horror. "'Tis possibly a portent of doom, Will!" he went on, pointing a trembling forefinger at the girls.

"The very opening of *The Globe* is threatened by this ill omen, Burbage," Shakespeare yelled, very close to tears.

"But, you are women!" rambled Burbage, very near to hysteria.

History had shown them many bizarre sights over the last few hours but this one - of two grown men in tights, fluffed pantaloons, frilled cuffs and slashed-sleeved doublets performing what could only be interpreted as some kind of Morris Dancing between the two pillars of the canopied stage - was way up in the top ten of extreme levels of weirdness. Shakespeare was crossing himself and tugging hard on his little beard whilst dancing a kind of Irish jig and Burbage was tugging his hat rim hard with his left hand and waving his short sword with his right - all the while turning in a tight figure of eight.

Short sword - wait a minute, wasn't that -

"The dagger!" yelped Chloe, excitedly, "That's our dagger!"

"Chronologically speaking, it is his dagger," Kira corrected whilst Shakespeare and Burbage leapt around as if they were on very hot coals, "We only borrow it. In - four hundred and twenty-two years' time."

"Quick maths," said a confused but impressed Chloe.

"All rounder, me," grinned Kira and turned her attention to the jigging Elizabethan actors. "Mister Shakespeare," she called, but the demented whirling continued. "Mister Shakespeare!" she repeated, a little louder, but still without success.

"MISTER SHAKESPEARE!" yelled Chloe at the top of her six-year-old lungs.

Shakespeare and Burbage stopped suddenly and looked at each other and then down at Kira and Chloe.

"You are *women*," repeated Burbage.

"Yes," said Kira.

"Nearly," said Chloe.

"And this means?" said Lucius.

"Thou art unfit for any place but - the yard!" shouted Shakespeare.

"Get thee to - the balcony!" cried Burbage - and the strange dance of the purification of superstitious Thespians continued.

"It would seem that they are afraid of you," said Lucius to Kira and Chloe.

"Master Shaxpee! Master Shaxpee!" called a new voice.

The actors stopped and looked out to the back of the circular theatre. Even though it was open to the sky above the yard, the balconies and therefore the entrances were protected by a thatched roof and it was hard to see who was calling from the outer shadows.

"Master Shaxpee!" it was another boy. He had run in from the street and clearly had some important news as he was clutching a grand looking, sealed scroll.

"That's Shakespeare, scullion!" shouted the exasperated playwright.

"Tis not what is written here," said the messenger boy as he passed Kira, Chloe and Lucius and climbed the stairs to the stage.

"Give me that," demanded Shakespeare, snatching the outstretched parchment tube and breaking the wax seal. He read aloud, "Masters Shaxpee, Burbage, Heminges, Phillips, Pope and the players of *The Lord Chamberlain's Men*. Be it not forgotten that I attend the final rehearsal of *Julius Caesar* this very afternoon - for to censor its content for the goodly benefit of Her most Glorious Majesty, Queen Elizabeth. Signed Edmund Tilney, Her most Regal Majesty's Master of the Revels." He paused, probably for dramatic effect, and then continued, "P.S. I would have a cushion for though your playhouse is new, I do fear those benches are most uncomfortably bedecked with splinters."

"A cushion!" roared Burbage, "Why, the very nerve of that knave."

"With great respect, Burbage, 'tis not the cushion that should cause us grief but Tilney himself - he will be here shortly," reasoned Shakespeare.

"Pish! Tilney is as tedious as a tired horse," alliterated Burbage.

Shakespeare was visibly terrified, "*Sir* Edmund Tilney is the Master of the Revels - 'tis his job to say whether the play is of suitable quality. He comes here to view our very livelihood and will discover an incomplete playhouse, an incomplete company of players and - a stage full of wenches!" Shakespeare threw an angry glare to accompany his violent finger pointing at Kira and Chloe. The messenger boy stood open-mouthed next to him, incomprehensible at the sight of girls in front of him.

Seeing his disbelief, Burbage lied, "They are but boys."

"Boys?" questioned the messenger.

"Aye, boys - men that lack height and beards!" clarified Shakespeare, "Get thee hence, minion."

All the while staring incredulously at the two girls, the messenger descended from the stage and crossed the theatre yard.

Kira found her courage again. "I take it that it isn't common to see women actors?" she asked.

"Ye gods!" bellowed Burbage, "Where hast thou been! Knowest thou not the law? Never!"

"Never?" asked Chloe.

"'Tis unacceptable in polite society," clarified Shakespeare.

"'Tis sexist," complained Kira, in period-style.

Burbage and Shakespeare were about to list the many essential reasons for there being no women allowed on the stage when there was a loud thumping on one of the theatre doors.

"Burbage?" came a shout from the street outside.

"Tilney," Burbage said in an equally loud stage 'whisper'.

"Shaxpee?" called Tilney through the closed oak doors.

"Will no-one remember my name?" moaned Shakespeare.

"Open your doors for Her Gracious Majesty's Master of the Revels," Tilney demanded from the Southwark streets outside.

"Methinks, our revels now are ended," muttered Shakespeare, his face dropping dejectedly.

"Peace, Will, peace," Burbage said, calmly, "To the purpose." Shakespeare looked to Burbage for his inspiration and a well-drafted plan. All the while, Tilney's shouts became louder and more urgent. "The company is readying for the performance in the tiring room," Burbage continued to Shakespeare, completely ignoring Tilney.

"Aye," agreed Will.

"Shaxpee! Shaxpee!" yelled Tilney in between continued door battering.

"Could he not just call me Will?" pleaded Shakespeare.

"We shall conceal these wenches in the tiring room," Burbage went on, oblivious to Shakespeare's worries about his surname, "This minion shall play the part of Lucius." Burbage was indicating the real Lucius. "And Tilney will be satisfied and grant us right to perform," he finished.

"Aye?" wavered Shakespeare.

"Aye!" assured Burbage.

"These players - are they all in bed!" roared Tilney, drawing a great deal of interest from the other actors who had started to appear in the various entrances at the back of the stage.

"You want us to hide?" asked Chloe.

"Aye!" agreed Shakespeare and Burbage simultaneously.

"Through there?" Chloe continued as she pointed to the back wall of the stage.

"Aye!" they nodded, together again.

"You want Lucius to act?" Kira asked.

"Aye!" the pair enthused with a little desperation.

"That's a lot of 'Ayes'," Kira smiled.

"Well?" pleaded Shakespeare as Tilney's shouted demands had reached crescendo, "What say you?"

Kira had been thinking about getting her hands on the dagger - though Max would never have believed her, he had never been out of her thoughts since they had lost him in Ancient Rome. Now, she was going to drive a bargain, "He must consult with his agent," she said and took Lucius and Chloe a few steps further away from the two distressed actors.

"You have a plan," Chloe informed her sister with a smile of realisation.

"Of course," she pushed her *clever spectacles* to the bridge of her nose and whispered to Chloe and Lucius, "Lucius will act." She could see Lucius wavering over this idea - after all, he must have known of actors from the Amphitheatres of Rome but clearly thought he wasn't capable. Kira consoled him to relax his troubled expression, "It's alright, Lucius, you will act for a suitable reward." Lucius looked even more confused. "We will negotiate your Thespian skills as part of an exchange for the dagger that Burbage has - the key to getting you home and rescuing Max," Kira finished and watched Lucius' face light up with the promise of a return trip home.

"I will go back to Rome?" he said in disbelief.

"Yeah," smiled Kira, "Yeah, you will."

"Then I will try this - acting," agreed Lucius.

"Brilliant," clapped Chloe with great excitement.

The three youngsters looked back to the two Elizabethan players. Both of them were used to an audience knowing more than the characters on stage but never had it been truer than it was at this very moment as they looked back at the children in the yard.

"What say you, Miss?" asked Burbage.

"Have we found a 'Lucius'?" pleaded Shakespeare.

"Oh, I can do better than that," grinned Kira with the upper hand, "You have found *the* Lucius!"

There was louder knocking from the playhouse doors again. It sounded like Tilney had summoned re-enforcements.

"Open up, I say, or - by the gods - there will be no play!" Tilney cried.

"Quickly!" panicked William Shakespeare, "Things do get worse, for he has started to rhyme."

Burbage gave a curt nod to a fellow actor at the back of the stage and indicated that he should let the irate Tilney into *The Globe*. The actor nodded back and crossed the stage to leave it via the steps and head to the outer doors. Meanwhile, Shakespeare had scurried to an old table just inside the middle door at the rear of the stage and returned with a sheet of parchment.

"Sir, your copy," he said and handed the sheet to Lucius.

Kira stepped in front of Lucius to make her demand. "On one condition," she stated.

"Anything," agreed Burbage, "Anything - but later. Here, Tilney comes. You must conceal yourselves."

"To the tiring room. I pray you make haste," said Shakespeare, his nerves obviously jangling.

Kira and Chloe were half guided, half dragged into the room at the back of the stage through the middle doorway by the frantic Elizabethan playwright. This was the tiring room where you would put on your 'attire' for a performance. Glancing back in a reassurance to Lucius, they could just make out the irritated figure of Sir Edmund Tilney, Master of the Revels. He was round faced - now red with anger - and wore black. Shoes, tights, doublet and hose, long sleeveless, fur-trimmed gown and a hat that looked a little like a squashed pie - all black. He was accompanied by two armed soldiers; clearly expecting trouble from the Bear Baters, Cock Fighters, Players and other assorted undesirables south of the river Thames.

"By the heavens, why was I left out there in the muddy ditches of Southwark?" Tilney complained as loudly as he had shouted.

"'Twas a minor problem with the doors, my Lord," interjected Burbage quickly, "Truly, my lord, they were unfortunately most bedecked with splinters." Tilney, though important, was not the brightest star in Elizabeth's Court and completely missed Burbage's dig at him. "Indeed, we feared for your Lordship's very gloves."

"Indeed," said Tilney, looking around him at the tiered balcony seating and open yard, "So this is *The Clove*, eh?"

"*The Globe*, yes," corrected Burbage, "And all is ready."

"You have worked from the allowed book?" Tilney asked as more of a demand than a request.

"But, of course," Burbage bowed with a sycophantic flourish.

"Then I will see the performance; lest it be unsuitable for the delicate senses of the Queen." Tinley seemed satisfied and fortunately - for the future of *The Globe* - unaware at the sniggering of many an actor behind the scenes. *The Lord Chamberlain's Men* had played many times for Queen Elizabeth and been witness to her tantrums, her interruptions and her raucous laughter at some of the comic scenes - delicate senses, she most certainly did not have.

Burbage was in full flattering mood, "I pray you, my most gracious Lord, do take a seat whilst we ready ourselves for *The most Excellent Tragedy of Julius Caesar.*"

Tilney ordered his soldier accompaniment to follow him to a seat in the lower gallery level with the stage. He glanced around him as he prepared to sit. The stage was fairly impressive - open to the elements, it had a dark blue canopy fretted with the stars of the heavens covering the rear section and two ornately decorated pillars about a third of the way back from the front. Those unlucky enough to stand in the yard for a performance may only have paid a penny but ran the risk of a soaking from the unpredictable London weather. In the galleries, continued dryness was assured on account of the thatched roof covering them. Tilney lowered himself to his seat -

"Wait!" he suddenly stopped sitting and shouted, "Wait I say!"

Actors appeared again and Burbage took centre stage, fearing Tilney had had a terrible accident.

"My Lord Tilney?" Burbage asked.

"This play shall not proceed!" Tilney was suddenly outraged.

"My Lord?" questioned Burbage.

"Without my cushion!" demanded Sir Edmund.

Burbage breathed a sigh of relief then, realising how demanding Tilney had been, was about to give him a piece of his mind. Luckily for *The Globe*, Shakespeare returned and provided the instant distraction.

"Ah, Shaxpee," Tilney greeted the playwright.

"*Please* call me Will, my Lord," Shakespeare winced at this 'other' version of his surname.

"On the arrival of my cushion, I will see the play," announced Tilney, at his most pompous yet.

"Of course, Sir Edmund," Shakespeare responded through a gritted smile then turned to Burbage with a very real one.

"Why dost thou grin, Will? Where hast thou been?" berated Burbage - as if cross at being left with Tilney alone.

"Engaged in the disguise of the two young wenches, Richard," he said animatedly.

"Disguise, Will?" Burbage was a little worried. Shakespeare had proved all too fond of dressing characters as other characters in his various, and some would say over complicated, comedies. There was no time for this afternoon to descend into a pleasantry of mistakes.

"Aye, Burbage, they are disguised - as boys," Shakespeare was beside himself with his ingenuity.

"Thou hast a thing about cross-dressing, Will," Burbage said in disbelief, "'Tis not one of your comedies. Would it not have been easier just to hide them?"

"Well -" Shakespeare was beginning to see a few flaws in his own enthusiasm, "Shall we just begin?"

Noting that the cushion had been delivered and that Tilney was shuffling like a hen repositioning over precious eggs, Shakespeare gave word for the performance to start. There was the flourish of a fanfare and the stage was cleared to begin.

From the dingy back stage tiring room Kira could hear the famous opening lines of *Julius Caesar* and it suddenly struck her that they had been involved in this very scene before - they had been part of the real events that took place one thousand six hundred and forty-three years ago - earlier this afternoon. The angry crowd was there; the two helpless senators; the overall mood that something big was about to happen. If only she could tell Mr. Speed, her English teacher, that she had been to see a performance of *Julius Caesar* at *The Globe* - in 1599. Her thoughts crashed down around her as she imagined the raucous laughter from the rest of her form. She then knew that claiming that she had done some *original research* on the period that the play was set in would prove even more disastrous to her reputation as a teenager. Then, there was her current clothing. Shakespeare had been very keen to disguise the two sisters. Kira looked at Chloe in her Elizabethan page boy attire - with her hair gathered underneath her large cap, she would convincingly have passed as a young lad. However, Kira in a man's doublet and hose left a lot more to be desired - and as for the fake beard tied with thread around the back of her head and proving to be extremely itchy - no-one would be convinced that she were anything but a girl in an Elizabethan man's clothing.

Lucius was staring at the manuscript page in his hand, unsure of what he should be doing. Burbage entered the darkness of the tiring room from the stage, cursing the carpenter as he cracked his head on the low door beam. Rubbing his head and cursing some more, he noticed Lucius and was remarkably perceptive in his understanding of the situation.

"Methinks, the words do trouble thee, lad," he said in an almost fatherly way as he sat down on the bench with Lucius. "Ah. 'Tis always the way as a player. Come, I will help thee."

Thus it was that a famous Elizabethan actor helped a little known Roman slave to learn the lines to play himself in a play about one of Rome's greatest events. It was rather touching and soon ended in smiles and hugs as Burbage demonstrated the right gestures and postures, entrances and exits. Burbage was so successful as an acting coach that when it came to Lucius' scenes, he was a natural. The same could not be said for Kira and Chloe.

In a desperate attempt to bolster the numbers and add realism to the crowd scenes of Ancient Rome, Shakespeare had dragged and pushed the two girls into various places and given complex directions to enable them to *enhance* the action. That was exactly what they didn't do. Chloe immediately walked off the edge of the stage on account of her large hat slipping over her eyes. The fall, of easily a metre and a half, could have really hurt if it hadn't been for a rather surprised carpenter who caught her as he chiselled fresh decoration into the woodwork below. Undeterred, she was lifted safely back on, smiling in embarrassment. Then Kira created a new scene - historically fashion conscious to the last, she bent to adjust her wrinkling tights and acted as the perfect stumbling block for the actor playing Cassius. In the middle of his powerful speech about how Caesar 'doth bestride the narrow world like a colossus' he backed away from Burbage's Brutus and did the most perfect backwards somersault over Kira. Face down on the stage, he was indeed able to 'peep about' between actors' legs - in a dishonourably grave situation.

The disasters continued: fake beard caught on scenery; Chloe waving recognition to Lucius like she did in her Primary School plays to Mum and Dad; fake beard caught in another actor's doublet; Chloe making several grabs at Burbage's dagger; fake beard caught in a scroll as Kira delivered a message; utter confusion when Kira's low battery alert refused to stop beeping leading to a mass stage evacuation due to 'witchcraft'; fake beard caught fire from the real candles used to let the audience know it was night and best of all - Kira's final scene. She had been instructed by Shakespeare to play the role of Strato - the Roman soldier who held Brutus' sword as he threw himself onto it to avoid the humiliation of capture. She dutifully took the sword from the brilliantly emotional Burbage, dropped it, kicked it hard off the stage whilst trying to pick it up and accidentally stabbed the scenic artist putting the finishing touches to the highly decorative stage front. Dismissed as a 'mere flesh wound' by Burbage, it had taken three very tight tourniquets to prevent the new stage from being tinged crimson.

After an age, the curtain call arrived. Tilney stood and applauded furiously, grinning from ear to ear.

"Master Shaxpee, you have excelled yourself!" he gushed,

wiping tears from his eyes.

"Shakespeare, Master Tilney," corrected Burbage.

Shakespeare leaned to Burbage and whispered, "He likes it, he may call me whatsoever he wishes."

Tilney continued in his exuberant praise, "Most excellent, Shaxpee!"

Shakespeare was truly taken aback. Tilney had seen many of his works and had barely managed a grunt before leaving with the most modest of nods of approval. "Truly, you are too kind, Master Tilney," he bowed in thanks.

Tilney continued to applaud - tears rolling down his face, he chuckled, "'Twas the best *comedy* I have seen this very year!"

It was a little like a slap in the face with a tanner's apron; and one that had just been used during the process of curing animal skins in urine - at that. Shakespeare's jaw dropped. "Comedy, Sir Edmund?" he squeaked.

"Aye, Shaxpee. Truly, those two boys - those two clowns did make the history come to life," Tilney was now almost hyper-ventilating with laughter.

Shakespeare's look was murderous and Kira was sure that he would use this moment as a reference point for the motivation of murderous tyrants in his future plays. "Those two boys!" he spat.

Burbage leaned to Will and said, "Did I not mention that they should merely have been hidden?"

Tilney had left the lower gallery and was waving his cushion excitedly, "And not one splinter!" He launched the cushion and hit Shakespeare square in the face. That was the final blow. It took every ounce of effort for William Shakespeare to remain on stage with his hands at his side and not tightening around Tilney's neck.

"I am so pleased, Master Tilney," Shakespeare lied, manically.

"And so will be Her Most Gracious Majesty," giggled Tilney as he turned to leave, "Your appearance at court is certain, Shaxpee."

Shakespeare watched him go and listened to various chuckles and remembered lines - 'Et tu Brute', 'Beware the Ides of March', 'Friends, Romans, Countrymen' all delivered with the sighs of recovering from extreme hilarity.

"Will no-one understand my plays?" Shakespeare whimpered.

Burbage clapped Shakespeare in between the shoulder blades and cried, "Aye, Will, a hit. A very palpable hit!" Shakespeare looked up to Burbage, his top lip trembling in abject depression. Burbage continued, oblivious, "Methinks a visit to *The Mermaid*, Will."

Chloe was suddenly very animated, "Cool, I love Mermaids. Is she little?"

Burbage laughed heartily and said, "Zounds, thy words are strange, minion."

Kira wanted to know about mermaids too though and asked, "The Mermaid?"

"Our local hostelry," informed Burbage - but seeing blank faces from Kira, Chloe and Lucius, thought it better to elaborate, "Ah, the innocence of youth. The Tavern."

There was a general shout of approval from most of the actors and a forward surge towards the theatre doors. Burbage grabbed Shakespeare by the hand and dragged him, still numb, along with the players' fraternity. The children were alone and the noise was receding. Lucius looked to Kira, saying, "I am not sure where I am. Nor what I have just taken part in. Or even what kind of people are these. But if we are to get the dagger, we should visit this - temple of the Mermaid."

Kira smiled at Lucius. "I hope they liked your acting," she said, "Because I've got to barter for it."

Chloe tugged at Kira's doublet and said, grinning from little ear to little ear, "Not as much as they liked mine." Then, with the absolute brilliance of childhood innocence, said to Kira, "You know, that beard suits you. You should grow one when you're older."

Kira and Chloe laughed - laughed and hugged each other - and in that hug, realised there was something missing. It was their brother. They had been a good few hours in 1599 and got no closer to retrieving the key to Ancient Rome, for the dagger that killed Julius Caesar had just gone to the pub.

Chapter Fifteen

On their second back alley history tour of the day, Kira found herself preferring the sights, sounds and smells of Ancient Rome. The streets of London were certainly not paved with gold - as Dick Whittington had apparently been led to believe. In fact, they weren't paved at all - most were little more than rough country tracks and any covering they had was mainly organic and distinctly unpleasant. The timber framed buildings on either side of the streets leaned towards each other and thankfully blocked the light from illuminating exactly what it was that squished underfoot.

Burbage, Shakespeare and a handful of other players from *The Globe* were highly skilled at avoiding alleyway hazards and very alert to the shouts of "Gardyloo!" from the windows above as people emptied chamber pots into the streets below. Hygiene seemed to have given Elizabethan London a miss and Kira was extremely grateful when she spotted the sign for *The Mermaid*. The narrow inn jutted a little further into the street than the other buildings; perhaps to catch unsuspecting travellers who hadn't realised they needed refreshment.

Not that Kira would have eaten or drank anything served inside. The straw hewn and very uneven floor was dotted with an oddment of furniture, barrels and crates serving as tables and seating. Pipe smoke hung thick in the air thanks to Sir Walter Raleigh's recent contribution to the health of the Nation - Virginia tobacco - and various forms of animal life scuttled and ran beneath peoples' feet. Kira counted rats, mice and shrews for her rodent spotters badge and began to see why the Plague would find it so easy to kill a hundred thousand people in sixty-six years' time. Again, all this seemed to go unseen by the group of actors who roared their way in to the tavern with raucous greetings and shouts of acknowledgement.

Shakespeare, caught up in the wave of conviviality, stopped

suddenly. "Pish," he complained as he heard a voice much louder than the rest and then spotted its owner, "Ben Jonson, the only man in London who could start a riot in an empty room." Kira, Chloe and Lucius followed Shakespeare's gaze to a younger, auburn-haired and thick-set man seated nearby. He sported the customary Elizabethan facial hair in the form of a pointed beard and was dressed in a dark green velvet doublet with a short blue cape draped over his left shoulder.

"Why, who better to keep our spirits raised," cried Burbage and strode across to the extremely loud Jonson.

"Burbage!" roared Ben Jonson in recognition, spilling his ale as he thumped his tankard onto the barrel that served as his table. "Shirksbeard!" he cried to Will who cringed at yet another version of his surname.

"Sit ye down, lads, sit ye down," Jonson gestured to a couple of crates and a rough looking plank wedged onto two smaller barrels. Burbage sat eagerly, Shakespeare sat reluctantly and Kira, Chloe and Lucius stood self-consciously. "More ale here. More ale, I say!" Jonson looked across to his pale and gaunt drinking companion and added, "George will collect the tab."

The pale man lifted a hand to argue, managing, "But-" before being interrupted by the red-haired and ruddy faced Jonson.

"But of course you will, George," he boomed, "Well this is pleasant - is it not? We should come here more often."

"You do, Jonson," said George, "Every evening."

"What say you, George?" asked a suddenly subdued Jonson.

"And lunchtime," George added.

"Verily, George, 'tis where I find my muse!" Jonson quipped, to the laughter of - himself, mainly. Calming slightly, he changed the subject and turned his attention to Shakespeare, "'Tis good you should join us this very night, Strangerear, for George Chapman and I were discussing the qualities of tragedy and comedy."

"Really," muttered Shakespeare, smarting from another surname snipe.

"Aye. We could not decide which were the better - *my* tragedies or *my* comedies!" Jonson roared with laughter. Shakespeare lowered his head and shook it from side to side slowly. He had tolerated this new upstart to the London stage for a few years now but was not sure how much longer he could suffer his company. "Methinks *Julius Caesar* doth not go well," Jonson sneered.

Burbage jumped to Shakespeare's defence, "Nay, nay, Jonson. It was right well received by Master Tilney this very afternoon."

Shakespeare looked dejected, in spite of his friend's support, and Chloe found herself standing next to him and rubbing his arm to make him feel better. Kira smiled at her caring nature.

"Tilney? Pish! He doth have little taste," spat Jonson through a mouthful of ale, wiping his beard free of bubbles with the back of his hand.

"As I do recall, Jonson," smiled Burbage, "He did *adore* thy last play,"

Jonson faltered - the wind temporarily blown from his sails, "Aye, well, Burbage - every rule must have an exception."

"Especially where you are concerned, Benjamin," added Burbage.

"What, Burbage? What meanest thou by that?" Johnson was rattled, "That my dramatic works be somewhat inferior?"

Shakespeare raised his head then quickly turned to the children. "We should conceal ourselves yonder," he said, pointing to the grey oak bar.

"Why, sir?" asked Lucius.

"Jonson doth have the same nature as a gunpowder keg," Shakespeare added.

"Gunpowder keg?" questioned Chloe.

"Aye," Shakespeare explained, "Light the wrong fuse and he may well explode." Shakespeare ushered the three away, protectively, "I pray you, retire to safety, young ones."

From the relatively safe distance of the bar, the children and the Elizabethan playwright watched the argument between Jonson and Burbage gather momentum. Barrels were scattered, jaws were squared, honour was threatened and finally - swords were drawn. Suddenly, Jonson's intent to fight was distracted as he set eyes upon Burbage's dagger.

"'Tis a somewhat fancy sword, Burbage!" he spat.

"It's there!" cried Chloe from across the smoke-filled tavern.

"I see it," said Kira, "Shhh." Kira hoped that a struggle might follow and in it, the dagger could be retrieved - somehow. It wasn't to be for actor and dramatist were suddenly engaged in a discussion about antiques.

"What, this old thing?" Burbage was saying, "'Twas from *The Rose* playhouse. 'Twas one of the props. I did *borrow* it from the Props Master there. He said there was much interest in it."

"Really?" Jonson was sheathing his own dagger and regarding Burbage with something akin to jealousy.

"Indeed," continued Burbage, "I am expecting the arrival of an expert on matters of antique artefacts with a view to making myself a few sovereigns." Burbage patted the purse hanging from his belt.

Kira was suddenly very alarmed. It seemed that whenever the dagger appeared and offered them a glimmer of hope of a return to their lost brother, it was swiftly removed from their reach and sent on a further journey.

"He's going to sell it," Kira hissed to Chloe and Lucius through her fake beard.

"He can't," gasped Chloe.

"We must get it back - before he sells it," reasoned Lucius.

"We have to think quickly," Kira was beginning to panic. She had started today as a calm and collected girl of fourteen - perhaps a little paranoid about her appearance but still relatively normal - but now, she didn't even know when today had begun. It had, after all, already lasted several millennia.

Burbage was bragging about the dagger, "He did say it was a special sword."

Jonson's admiration now quickly turned to scorn, "In that it is a bit - flamboyant, Burbage? A bit womanly!"

Shakespeare had seen these altercations many times before. He had even been involved in some of the early brawls - the black eye he had sported for his role as King Henry in the second part of *Henry IV* had received rave reviews. Later though he had become content to observe; to observe and pray that Burbage wasn't injured. Without Richard Burbage, there would be no plays, for he was very much admired as an actor. The argument continued but, as yet, had not reached blows.

"New players, Will," said Mistress Snell, the owner of *The Mermaid* who had slid a tankard of ale on the bar in front of Shakespeare and was pointing to the children. Shakespeare, still watching the posturing of Burbage and Jonson looked wearily at her. She smiled warmly and wiped her ale drenched hands on her leather apron. "Hath *The Lord Chamberlain's Men* new members, Will? Yonder bearded lad hath a goodly aspect," she enthused, winking favourably at Elizabethan Kira.

Shakespeare was quick to give her his full attention, "Thou canst stop that right there, Mistress Snell. Truly, go not there - all is not what it seems."

"Thou dost talk in riddles, Will," she laughed, "What meanest thou with that?"

"Just that *she* is but - a lad," he said, somewhat carelessly.

"She?" Mistress Snell was confused.

"He, sorry," Shakespeare hoped he had diverted her attention and, indeed, it appeared that Burbage had diverted Jonson's too. Somehow, Jonson was now slapping Burbage broadly on the back and laughing heartily.

"Right," Jonson roared, "Who's for a game of *One and Thirty*?" There was a considerable lack of interest in this offer but Jonson was not deterred, "What, dare'st thou not play me, Ben Jonson, Master of the Cards?"

Again there was little response, until the small, pale George Chapman decided to declare his irritation, "No, they dare'st not play thee, Ben Jonson, Master of the Cheats."

For a moment, there was silence. However, Ben Jonson was not known for remaining silent for long. "You accuse me of the lowly act of cheating?" he boomed.

"Not accuse, Jonson. We know," laughed Burbage.

Out came Jonson's sword again as he cried, "Best be prepared for a damn good drubbing, Burbage!"

Mistress Snell often had the upper hand - as Landlady of a tavern in Southwark, loud and drunken actors, playwrights and other self-acclaimed creative persons were part of her way of life - and so it was that her upper hand came crashing down, holding an empty bottle, on Jonson's head and ending his tirade. She had had enough bluster for one afternoon and, deciding to use a well practiced technique, had chosen to give the other guests a break. Jonson slid to the floor accompanied by a general cheer and Mistress Snell's quip of, "Your usual, Master Jonson."

Burbage laughed heartily and looked to his greatest friend, Shakespeare, to see his reaction. It was not what he expected to see. Far from enjoying Jonson's temporary downfall, William Shakespeare didn't appear to have noticed. Concerned, Burbage crossed the straw covered floor to join him and the children at the edge of the bar.

"Come now, Will, surely that has raised your spirits?" pleaded Burbage.

"'Tis just that I fear that no one doth understand my work," Shakespeare replied, sullenly.

Kira was about to add that the situation was pretty much the same four hundred years later in classrooms and drama studios across the world but thought the concept of time travel combined with a further insult may well finish him off. Mistress Snell had overheard them and offered her interpretation. "Oh, come now, Will," she said, "I have seen and enjoyed everything thou hast done. Thou art right clever, Will."

Shakespeare raised a slight smile. "You believe so?" he asked.

"Aye, Will. *The Two Gentlemen of Verruca*," she offered.

"Verona," corrected Shakespeare.

"*The Straining of the Stew*," she went on.

"*The Taming of the Shrew*, yes," corrected Shakespeare.

"*A Comedy of Herrings*," she added.

"Errors," corrected Shakespeare.

"Oh, and not forgetting that one about the Jew," she queried.

"Aye, *The Merchant of Venice*?" said Shakespeare, proudly.

"No. What was it called - *The Jew of Malta* that was it. Brilliant that one," she concluded.

"That was by Christopher Marlowe," corrected Burbage.

William Shakespeare could take no more. Today, he had performed a comic rendition of his historical tragedy of *Julius Caesar* in an unfinished playhouse to end up being told that the play most appreciated in *The Mermaid* was written by someone else - someone unable to write more, on account of his death five years ago. "Oh, I give up," he sulked, "Nothing will come of this play writing," and he was gone. Quickly exiting followed by Burbage.

"Will?" called Burbage as he strode after him. However, he did not get as far as the door because out of the Virginia tobacco clouds stepped a somehow familiar figure.

"Master Burbage," he said.

"Sir Walter," Burbage nodded his greeting.

"Sir Walter!" cried Kira and Chloe together - and it was; it absolutely was Sir Walter Cope, Knight of Queen Elizabeth's College of Antiquaries and owner of Kensington Castle - but he was only about thirty years old and dressed in contemporary doublet and hose in a deep blue velvet. His long hair was black and lustrous and a neat dark goatee beard sat sharply on his chin. Kira quickly worked it out; that Sir Walter must have collected the dagger here, in *The Mermaid Inn* when he was a much younger man. If he was here to collect it now then they had to act quickly. The dagger could go who knows *when* if Sir Walter were to take it from Burbage.

"We have to get that dagger now," insisted Kira, "We can't let Sir Walter leave with it. It could be taken anywhere in history and we wouldn't know. Max and Lucius would be stuck in the wrong lives forever."

The seriousness of the situation struck Chloe. "Leave it to me," she said bravely, "If I don't come back, tell Mum and Dad I did everything to save Max."

She was serious. Kira had a lump in her throat and tears welled in her eyes as little Chloe hugged her and turned to go. "Chloe, what are you doing?" she called. Chloe was determined to make a difference and was working her way towards Burbage and the youthful Sir Walter.

"Do you have the dagger, Richard?" Sir Walter was asking.

"But of course, my Lord," Burbage replied, puzzled with the intensity of his request.

"The Queen will pay you handsomely for it, Richard," continued young Sir Walter with a somewhat mysterious air.

"'Tis but a prop, my Lord," said Burbage.

"No, Richard, 'tis much more than a prop. The Queen believes it to be imbued with special ability. She has assembled her finest alchemists -" Sir Walter paused, "Ah, but I fear that I have said too much." He held up a large bag which clearly contained Burbage's monetary reward. "The dagger, Richard," he requested.

Eyes wide at the sight of possible riches, Burbage reached for the dagger, "It is here, My Lord -" but it wasn't. Nimbly and largely unseen, Chloe had squeezed her way through the crowded inn and lightened Richard Burbage of the load of the dagger that killed Julius Caesar. For the third or fourth time today, pandemonium broke out.

"Run, Chloe!" yelled Kira, seeing what was happening.

"Zounds!" blasphemed Burbage as he saw the dagger being carried away and the bag of money being put away, "The minion has stolen my dagger."

"And without the dagger, Richard, there is no deal," chastised Sir Walter, disappearing slowly into the foul air, "The Queen will be mightily displeased when she hears of this."

Sir Walter was gone. Chloe and the dagger were gone. Kira and Lucius were in hot pursuit and confusion was the order of the moment. Burbage standing amidst the action thought for a moment then yelled, "Once more unto the breach, dear friends, once more." Burbage was gone from *The Mermaid* too. Never had a mere dagger been given so much importance - except perhaps Excalibur.

Chapter Sixteen

History, it seemed, was quite dangerous - although there were guns and weapons of mass destruction in the 21st Century, there seemed to be fewer individuals with access to them there. Here and now - actually deep within History, struggles, fights, skirmishes and death were major constituent ingredients of the 16th Century. All about them were men armed with swords and daggers, desperate beggars, cutthroats, thieves and vagabonds. They were in a strange city - one that they would be familiar with in four hundred and twenty-two years' time - but the Elizabethan London that they found themselves running through, was as alien as could be.

"We are probably looking for a flag," shouted an unsure Kira whilst running at full pelt.

"What sort of flag?" asked Chloe, sword in hand as if to cut her way through the crowded, narrow streets.

"I can't remember," Kira called, unhelpfully, "They flew flags from the theatres to advertise the performances - I think. Different flags for different shows. There can't be many tall buildings at this time. Just a few churches - so a flag pole should be visible on the skyline." Kira really wished that they had been able to take a leisurely ride on the London Eye to get their bearings but there was nothing at all leisurely about their hunt for the quick route back to *The Globe*. Kira knew that Burbage would be after them for what he thought was *his* sword and he had the distinct advantage of knowing any possible short cuts.

"There!" called Lucius pointing to his right, "It is Hercules!" He was right, a blue flag fluttered high above the relatively low skyline of Southwark and on it was the image of Hercules carrying - a globe. That had to be more than coincidence. Kira changed direction, taking an alley to her right and calling for the other two to follow her lead.

They rounded a tight corner and there it stood. In the warm afternoon sun of mid June, it looked magnificent. Clean white - washed walls, with neat shuttered windows about two thirds of the way up, sat in grey timber framing and towered over the rutted streets of scruffy Southwark to form a near circular structure. A neat thatched roof capped those walls and overflowed to the two turrets that jutted from the main circle of the theatre - one of these proudly held the flag that they had been following. Having seen the reconstructed version in modern London, Kira would have been happy to report that the architects and Shakespearean experts had got the new Globe just about right - before she was taken away for 'tests' by men in white coats, that is. Several entrances were visible, each with large double oak doors that had faded to the same silvery-grey.

For a moment, Kira breathed in the atmosphere of the place. It really was one of adventure and excitement - of a creative struggle to win the hearts of the penny-paying London audience. This was what studying Shakespeare in the 21st Century was lacking - Shakespeare's plays weren't just clever words to be read but powerful, age-old stories of human struggles to be experienced. Kira was caught up in something magical and light-years from the dry academic view of English Literature.

Chloe was staring at her. "Are we going in?" she asked, impatiently.

"Of course," answered Kira as she snapped out of her, quite profound, thoughts.

"Which door?" asked Lucius.

"Whichever one opens and lets us in," said Kira with a smile. Without letting on, she had seen that the nearest entrance doors were ajar and took the initiative to approach them. Kira was experiencing real tension with door opening these days - after all, until today, she had taken to expecting that if you were in a Tudor residence and you opened a Tudor oak door, you would find yourself in another Tudor room in that Tudor residence. Even if that door had a sign saying 'No Entry'. Tentatively, she pushed the solid oak door and it swung slowly inwards.

Whatever she thought of studying Shakespeare in a classroom, this was nothing short of magical. Entering under the first gallery at ground level, the three youngsters stepped into the shadows but were guided by bright light. June sunlight streamed in through the open centre and illuminated the new-built splendour of the playhouse and, as they stepped into the sunlit yard, the grandeur of it all was quite overwhelming. Three young people felt very small indeed in the centre of the round theatre with three galleries looking down upon them and a beautifully painted stage-front at Kira's head height in front.

Chloe broke the silence. "All clear?" she asked in a forced whisper.

"Deserted," answered Kira looking down at Chloe to ask, "Dagger?"

"Check!" she waved the sharp weapon and nearly had Lucius' eye on it. Lucius, however, did not even flinch as he stood in awe of this *temple* again. "Quill?" asked Chloe.

"Check!" said Kira as she pulled the white goose feather from the back pocket of her jeans.

"Plan?" asked Chloe.

"Hmmm," pondered Kira, "Lots of questions."

"About Sir Walter?" quizzed Chloe, expertly reading Kira's mind.

"He looked - much younger," Lucius was back in the yard in mind as well as body.

"Four hundred and twenty-two years younger, Lucius. I've got so many questions," Kira had such a lot of missing jigsaw pieces to this time-travelling puzzle that it had become frustrating.

"Yeah," said Chloe, "Me too. Like, how come they put so many black wine gums in a packet when nobody likes them?"

"I do not understand you, Chloe," muttered Lucius as she

added to his culture shock.

"Never mind, Lucius," said Kira, dismissing Chloe's innocent quest for knowledge, "At least one of us has a vague grip on some kind of reality." She held the quill in front of her face and twirled it slowly. "Back to the future?" she grinned - for out of the corner of her eye, she had seen it appear. The same, panelled oak door that had opened in three different millennia was shimmering, as if in intense heat, just under the gallery to their left and the goose feather quill was vibrating gently as if connected in some mysterious way.

Kira took Chloe's hand and Chloe reached for Lucius. Hand in hand, they opened the door and walked through.

When they had entered *The Globe*, they had thought it was deserted - but, it wasn't. Wide-eyed and open-mouthed sat William Shakespeare against the stage-left pillar. He had been wallowing in self-pity about the woes of being a misunderstood artist when the three children had entered and seemed to summon a doorway from the shadows. A doorway that was still there. He got to his feet. "Angels and ministers of grace defend us," he spluttered, making the sign of the cross and wishing that he had attended church on a few more Sundays. "Is this a doorway, which I see before me?"

William Shakespeare, Elizabethan playwright and poet, shareholder in *The Globe Theatre* and important member of the acting group called *The Lord Chamberlains Men*, jolted slowly down the stage steps and crossed the yard. He stood in front of the shimmering door with that warning 'No Entry' sign and slowly put his hand on the door handle - it was warm and buzzing slightly. Alarmed but determined, he opened the door and stepped through.

Chapter Seventeen

It had crossed Kira's mind that getting back to Kensington Castle in 2021 could be problematic. After all, they were using the quill - supposedly used by Shakespeare - as their return ticket but were also travelling with the dagger - that supposedly killed Julius Caesar. What if one were to interfere with the other? Would the dagger cancel out the quill and take them back to Ancient Rome? Or what if the collection date of both artefacts became some sort of equation or mathematical sum like - the oldest minus the youngest equals your new destination. That would mean minus forty four take away one thousand five hundred and ninety-nine. Kira couldn't remember how to use negative numbers in a sum and concealing the dagger under her doublet, abandoned that thought as she tore through the meeting point of two very different times and into a dark, panelled room.

There were shelves on all four walls from floor to high ceiling and all were filled with leather bound and clearly old books.

Kira steadied herself from her journey and said, "It looks like-"

She had no chance to finish as some of the very shelves of books opened as a concealed door and a somewhat bossy woman forced her way in. "The library," she announced proudly. It was the brown Tour Guide and she was soon accompanied by a familiar group of tourists who now looked to be suffering from extreme tedium. In fact, many looked barely alive. Kira spotted Mum and Dad, they were now a row back and even they had lost some of their enthusiasm. The Tour Guide started again, "This room was one of the first to be restored and holds a remarkable collection of first printings and rare manuscripts like -"

She had paused for dramatic effect. Had she looked closely at her tour group, she would have noticed a figure slip from behind Kira, Chloe and Lucius to blend in with the others. It didn't work

- he stood out like a sore thumb.

"Shakespeare!" cried Kira, Chloe and Lucius together, spotting the Elizabethan in the room. Now there was a dramatic effect.

"Indeed, you clever young things!" said the Tour Guide, completely missing the reason for the outburst and assuming they were just being surprisingly knowledgeable. "We have an extensive library of many of the first folio printings of Shakespeare's plays. So nice to see youngsters interested in something other than their portable textaphones and the interweb," she beamed, "So refreshing. Now, if you'd all care to follow me, the next room is particularly special." She paused again, perhaps waiting for sharp inhalations of anticipated breath, "Sir Walter's very own airing cupboard." The brown lady strode past, ruffling Lucius' hair and completely failing to notice his Roman-ness as she smiled on him. "Completed in fifteen hundred and ninety-eight in the very same oak quarter-sawn panelling, I bet you can all spot those flamed medullary rays by now, can't you?" She was gone and the first few members of the tour group shuffled off with her.

Kira felt like shouting, "Dead man walking!" as they passed lifelessly by.

Mr and Mrs Foster drew level with their daughters. "That's my girls!" said Dad, "Very clever!" He nodded to Lucius and said, "Oh, hello, Julian."

"Lucius," grumbled Chloe in disgust.

"Where's Max?" asked Mum.

"Toilet," said Kira.

"Again?" frowned Mum.

Kira nodded unconvincingly but Mum and Dad flowed past all the same, following the tour group. Leaving the room, Mum could be heard saying, "We'll have to take him to see Doctor Patterson. It isn't natural to go so many times in one day." Their parents were gone again.

"They are so rubbish!" Chloe announced again - as they had failed to notice Elizabethan costumes, a fake beard, a real Roman and William Shakespeare, she rested her case.

The last of the tour ambled by - but not Shakespeare, as Kira grabbed him by his arm and pulled him angrily back. "Not so fast, Shakespeare," she said with teeth clenched.

"By heaven, this is most wondrous strange," Shakespeare announced as he looked dizzily around at the library.

"You followed us!" accused Chloe.

"I was in *The Globe* and did see the magic doorway appear. I was transported here - this is - ?"

Shakespeare was interrupted by an irate Kira, "Great! Let's get ourselves a collection of genuine historical figures. Free with Part One - a genuine Roman slave boy; and coming in part two - your very own William Shakespeare," she paused and glowered. "Neither of you should be here!" she yelled.

"But this is a library," said Shakespeare, "And never have I seen such a collection." He picked a volume from the shelves by his right hand. "Ovid's *Metamorphoses*," he read the inside cover then picked off another, "Raphael Holinshead's *Chronicles*," and another, "Ser Giovani's *Il Pecorone*."

Kira fumed at the growingly complex situation that they were in. Shakespeare was oblivious in literary bliss. "Wait - *The Tragedy of Richard the Third* by William Shakespeare - spelled incorrectly but most definitely mine own work." He put down the larger volumes and opened the play copy with great reverence reading, "Now is the winter of our discontent made glorious summer by this son of York." Shakespeare stopped, closed the book and picked up another. "*Loves Labour's Lost* - my comedy!" he announced with a broad grin and moved to the next, "*The Most Excellent and Lamentable Tragedy of Romeo and Juliet* - a first printing. And *A Midsummer Night's Dream* - most excellent." Now, Shakespeare had an armful of books but still, he went for more. "And *Measure for Measure* by William Shakes-" he stopped suddenly and frowned, *"Measure for Measure?* 'Tis not mine. And *Macbeth?* Mine neither. And *The Tempest* also assigned to Master William Shakespeare!"

Shakespeare was confused but Kira had realised. "We need to stop him now," she whispered to Chloe and Lucius as Shakespeare had reached a collected version of his comedies, histories and tragedies, "In 1599, he hasn't written a lot of his most famous plays yet." Kira was quite distraught and, suddenly, so was Shakespeare. He had reached a first folio of his collected works, placed down the other plays, and was reading a dedication from the collection out loud.

"To the memory of Master William Shakespeare. We wondered, Shakespeare that thou went'st so soon from the world's stage to the grave's tiring room. We thought thee dead -" Shakespeare paused and Kira suddenly felt very responsible for showing William Shakespeare his own mortality. "James Mabbe. 1623. The year of Our Lord 1623? This cannot be so. 'Tis but 1599. 'We thought the dead'," Shakespeare stopped again and turned accusingly to the children. "Where is this place?" he asked.

"Try *when* is this place," Kira said, heavy with the knowledge that the understanding she would be asking of him was enormous.

"When?" he muttered.

"Yes, Shakespeare, *when,"* Kira paused before dropping the bombshell, "This is the year 2021."

Shakespeare was without words, "Two -"

"Thousand and twenty-one," finished Kira.

"You did speak of the future by the magic doorway," he mused.

"Yep. And you're in it!" said Chloe with all the subtlety of close-range cannon fire.

"'Tis impossible," snapped Shakespeare.

"I thought so too," added Lucius who was almost seeing the reality of the situation - even if he could not fully understand it.

"You are prepared to walk through a *magic doorway* though," said Kira accusatorily.

"Witchcraft?" asked Shakespeare.

"If you believe in that sort of thing," said Kira.

"'Tis very fashionable at the moment," he stopped and thought, "In 1599, it is very fashionable. So, this is - the future?"

Kira and Chloe nodded seriously to the playwright as he continued, brightly, "And these collected works that I know not of - *Measure for Measure, Macbeth* - they are my future works?"

Kira squirmed at the complex conversation she knew was coming, "Ah, you will write them. Yes."

"Truly? Then I am remembered?" Shakespeare's smile gleamed wider.

"More than that, Shakespeare, you are studied," Kira added.

"Studied?"

"In schools," Kira went on, "every child will study one of your plays."

"With my name correctly written?" Shakespeare realised the amazing situation he had found himself in and started unbuttoning his doublet to stuff the book of collected works inside, "Then, methinks, there is something to this play writing game after all!"

"What are you doing?" snapped Chloe, sensing that this was wrong.

"Why must I go to the trouble of constructing new works when they are here - already formed!" Shakespeare was ecstatic.

A dark shadow had moved across the floor as a man slipped silently into the library from the bookcase door. "I'm afraid that time doesn't work like that, Will," said Sir Walter Cope.

"Sir Walter," cried Shakespeare, taken aback by a now grey haired old man in an ornate coat, "Thou art - old!"

Sir Walter ignored Shakespeare for the moment and looked angrily to Kira and Chloe. "Things appear to be drifting further from the simple plan agreed, children," he said, rather threateningly.

"You can talk," said Kira sharply, "We saw you in 1599."

"I do see Sir Walter regularly at court, children. There is nothing in that - excepting that he doth now appear to be of great age." Shakespeare had realised half way through his sentence that things really were not as simple as they seemed.

"What is happening, Sir Walter?" asked Chloe.

Sir Walter sighed and everyone in the room could suddenly see the pain and suffering in his deep blue eyes. "It is complicated," he said, still stubbornly holding onto the key to a mystery.

"Please explain," pleaded Chloe as she looked up at the old man - and few people could resist the big dark eyes of a curious six-year-old.

"I will try," agreed Sir Walter and he sighed as if to unburden himself of the heaviest of loads, "I was born in the year 1553."

"But that would make you very old," Chloe thought aloud, "No, that would make you very - dead."

"So you're four hundred and sixty-eight years old," Kira quickly did the Maths.

"No, I am seventy-nine. That is I have lived for seventy-nine years," Sir Walter informed them all.

"How can you be seventy-nine, four hundred and sixty-eight years after you were born?" Kira was getting impatient now.

"I have been alive for seventy-nine years but, I am the victim of my wanderings. My wanderings in time and history - for I have not lived every single day between the year of my birth and now. I have lived the equivalent of seventy-nine years. Roughly seventy-nine years. I cannot be exact." Sir Walter looked really serious and he had confused everyone present.

"No," said Kira, not standing for anything less than a full explanation, "You will have to do better than that. There's a lot at stake here - We want to get our brother back, we need to take Lucius home and we absolutely need to get rid of Shakespeare." She threw an annoyed glance in the direction of the playwright, "And you are able to help us understand how to do it. Aren't you?" Kira could be very persuasive when she wanted something, almost threatening. "Aren't you?" she repeated through gritted teeth.

"Very well," Sir Walter sighed again and began to peel back some more of the layers of mystery shrouding his long life, "I was a successful man at court in 1599 and a mere forty-six years of age. I was a gentleman usher for Good Queen Elizabeth and I had constructed this house with family wealth from my inheritance and some good business dealings. I had married and had a family - and, as a distraction, I had started my collection of curiosities." To the others in the room, this seemed straightforward enough but Sir Walter suddenly became very dark indeed. His face creased in a frown and the others in the room watched several expressions chase across his features. "I was involved with something - greater," he paused and looked wistfully away for a moment, "Something far more dangerous and much darker. Something very secret - called Alchemy."

Lucius was pleased to have understood everything until the last word and determinedly asked, "Alchemy?"

"A powerful science, my lad. We were under instruction to discover *The Elixir of Life*," Sir Walter looked awkward - as if things in his story were about to turn bad.

"The what of life?" asked Chloe.

"We were charged to find the ultimate substance to put an end to disease and to prolong human lives. To make mankind immortal. To live forever," said Sir Walter, gravely.

"Ah, you mean The Philosopher's Stone," said Chloe cheerfully.

Sir Walter was genuinely taken aback, "You, child, understand the principles of Alchemy?"

"No," said Kira, "She has just seen the Harry Potter film." Chloe stuck her tongue out at Kira who smiled back then continued, "Who was it that instructed you to look for a cure for disease and ageing?"

"Queen Elizabeth herself. She was often ill and very afraid of her own mortality. In 1588, her Spy Master, Sir Francis Walsingham, had gathered together learned men to create *The College of Antiquaries* to examine the ancient mysteries of our world and gather artefacts with supernatural properties. We were to harness their power for the preservation of life, reign and kingdom. Amongst other supernatural happenings, he had received word of a mysterious dagger said to have been used to kill Julius Caesar. The Queen had spies everywhere but it took over ten years to find that dagger."

"It had, somehow, become the possession of the actor, Richard Burbage," added Kira.

Shakespeare smiled fondly and added, "He did always say 'twere a valuable little sword."

"You have no idea, Will," continued Sir Walter, "As a supporter of *The Lord Chamberlain's Men* and known to them all, I was sent to negotiate to buy the dagger for as much gold as was asked for."

"So the dagger does have special powers then?" Kira was thinking aloud.

"Not quite, it is truly a dagger, made famous by what it was actually used for and little else, and when I met Burbage in *The Mermaid Inn*, the exchange had already been agreed but the dagger was stolen from under our very noses."

"That was us," said Lucius, pleased to have understood so

much, "We stole the dagger."

"But that was this very afternoon," reasoned Shakespeare.

"No, Will. That was four hundred and twenty-two years ago," there was a silence as what Sir Walter was saying sank in, "Burbage and I followed the thieves to *The Globe* but they had vanished and there was no sign of the dagger. I did retrieve other artefacts though - and they were to have a catastrophic affect on the rest of my life."

Kira had suspicions as to what Sir Walter had found but she couldn't possibly have guessed what these artefacts would actually turn out to be. Sir Walter bid the three children and Shakespeare to follow him through the bookshelf doorway and they found themselves back in the Cabinet of Curiosities. Shakespeare stood wide-eyed in what Kira supposed he saw as a giant props store - she also noticed that he was carrying the first folio of his collected works and made a mental note to remove it from him as soon as she could. Sir Walter crossed to one of the overflowing tables and opened a draw. He removed a carefully wrapped bundle and, beneath brown paper revealed -

"Our clothes!" cried Chloe - and they were the very clothes removed by Kira and Chloe when Shakespeare had forced them to dress as Elizabethan boys. There were, however, still too many elements missing to solve this riddle. Kira had suspected that the dagger was the key - not the outfits that they had dressed in this morning.

Finally, Sir Walter was to reveal the last piece of the puzzle. "You see, it isn't just the object - the dagger, the quill or the clothes. It is something within this very room. A very power emanating here in Kensington Castle. When an object joins this collection, it is infused with a power to open - a gateway - a bridge - to wherever it was taken from and back again. A sort of corridor through the years. A bridge over time if you like. But it is not an exact power. Not a controllable power. It has no master. Instead, it has mastered me," he explained.

"But our clothes weren't part of the collection," said Kira, thinking that she could see a flaw to his explanation.

"I mused on this for many years but when I first set eyes upon you in the Cabinet of Curiosities, it all became clear. Chloe, my child, what were you doing when you first met me?" Sir Walter had a twinkle back in his eye and some of the weariness had lifted - he even looked a little younger.

"Nothing!" said Chloe defensively, "We didn't touch anything."

"Ah, but you did, Chloe. You and Max were trying on some of the items of historical interest and - you had taken off your outer garments to do so, placing them on this table."

"So they accidentally joined the collection whilst we were in Ancient Rome!" Kira could see it now - the item that had disrupted Sir Walter's very existence and catapulted him into the future - was Chloe's stripy cardigan with the multi-coloured metal buttons. Countless science-fiction films had used capsules, teleports, time-ships and immense whirling constructions - even a telephone box - to travel through time but, in reality, it was a six year-old girl's striped cardigan. "Don't you see, Chloe, when you removed your cardy and put it on this table, it gained the same power as the dagger - to enable the finder to travel to where it was collected. And, it was used here, in Kensington Castle in two thousand and twenty-one. You put it back on when we got back from Rome. When we lost Max. It was cold so you put your cardigan on and we left for Shakespeare's time." Kira was very pleased with herself. It didn't seem to make sense but it worked as crazy theories go.

Chloe's little face lifted, "And we took off our clothes to get changed for the comedy in the theatre!"

"Tragedy! Tragedy, forsooth!" blurted Shakespeare.

"Depends where you were sitting, I think," laughed Kira on top of her deductive game.

"When I went into the tiring room of *The Globe Theatre* and picked up these items of clothing, my first doorway appeared. An oak doorway like all these here but marked 'No Entry' and I have stepped through that door many times since. When I had plucked up enough courage to try to open it, I ended up here - on this very day but in what I eventually realised was my own house. You always return to this very time on this very day in this very house of my future family," Sir Walter added, casting a worried look at Shakespeare who had sulkily settled at a table and returned his attention to learning lines from his future plays.

"OK, I get that you could travel here using Chloe's cardigan but how did you travel anywhere else?" Kira really thought that there was no explanation to this particular question - the idea of time-travelling cardigans was truly making her head hurt.

"I experimented with your clothing and travelled back and forth between what I soon discovered was the year 2021 and mine own time of 1599. I quickly realised that it was the item that enabled this mysterious transfer and that it was between two fixed points that never altered so I brought some of my collection with me and was able to widen my travelling. Each item, when placed in this room, was given the ability to open a doorway to the place and time of its use. To the time when the item was important in some way. I travelled further back than fifteen hundred and ninety-nine and each time returned with more objects from more times and places around the world," Sir Walter stopped again and his face dropped once more, "And here is my curse - though the items will always return you to a fixed time at both ends of your journey, the time you spend in History comes from your *own* lifespan. It is easy to think that you will go and spend a few months in Ancient Egypt or Medieval Paris - however, when you return you may have been gone from where you left for no time at all but you have aged during the time that you have spent elsewhere. And thus, I have wasted my life increasing my collection to widen my travel ability. It seems, to my family and friends, that one moment I am in the latter years of my forties and the next, I appear to be almost eighty."

Sir Walter had indeed become the victim of his own curiosity. Tears had formed in his deep blue eyes as he struggled to finish his tale. "My curiosity has cost me my life - my life has gone because I was foolish enough to think that being away for months and being able to return to an exact spot in 1599 would make no difference. My greed for the collection of knowledge has cost me the comfort of an old age with the ones I love - for when I return to my own time, my life is almost spent and my family want nothing to do with the strangely old Sir Walter Cope."

There was a very long silence - only broken by a truly insensitive Shakespeare noting, "'Twould make a wondrous entertainment for the stage." Four pairs of eyes bore down on him and he slowly returned to a spot of self-appreciation by continuing to read his own un-written works.

"There's a problem here," said Kira with some urgency.

"A problem?" asked Chloe who could think of nothing else to add to make things more complicated.

"Yes, a problem. We are stuck in events and we have to be extremely careful how we proceed," Kira was looking more worried than she had done in a long time. Even more worried than when she had discovered that the broadband was offline when workmen had drilled through the cable to their house. "We have got ourselves into a sort of loop. Where do we take the dagger? We need it to get to Rome and it is supposed to kill Julius Caesar but how do we get back here if we have to leave it there and, wait a minute, we *did* leave it there with Max already. How does that work?"

Sir Walter looked on impassively and merely said, "You see, time is like a web - with strands of events and happenings that are all inter-connected. If you break the web you may lose a part of it and so change history for better or for worse - you can never tell. You must return everything to its rightful place and *hope* you can preserve that web."

This was a monumental ask - an enormous undertaking with so many questions to be answered. For Chloe and Lucius, there was an element of ignorance being bliss: Chloe was unable to worry about the grand scheme of things as she had her very young age to thank for not quite understanding; Lucius was unable to worry about the grand scheme of things as he had massive culture differences to thank for not understanding and Shakespeare was unable to worry about the grand scheme of things as he was too busy laughing at his own future jokes and marvelling at his own future characterisations.

"Right," said Kira, breaking into a cold sweat, "Right - Lucius must return to Rome so we can get Max back and we must leave the dagger there. No! We need the dagger to get back here but what about the fact that it is supposed to kill Julius Caesar and how on earth does it get to Elizabethan London?" Kira had gotten louder and louder during her reasoning out loud, "What if I get it wrong? What if the dagger doesn't stay in Rome and so Caesar doesn't die? What if I break the chain of events and can't fix them?"

Kira was desperate and Chloe could see it; so too could Lucius - he may have come from another time, place and way of life but he could still recognise distress.

"I trust you," said Chloe as she hugged her big sister.

"And so do I," added Lucius as he patted her arm in support.

It was just as well that Kira had the support of Chloe and Lucius as Sir Walter Cope had gone who knows when.

Chapter Eighteen

There was a literary technique to describe this sort of thing but Kira couldn't remember what it was called. Lightning flashed and thunder groaned and rumbled emphasising that Kira was terrified of making a mistake with what she thought she must do. If she put a foot wrong, the History she had learned in school could suddenly become obsolete. Julius Caesar could avoid death and become King of Rome if she couldn't work out how to make amends.

It was night time in Ancient Rome and something had gone very wrong. Another flash of lightning illuminated the faces of Chloe, Lucius and William Shakespeare and the white light bounced from the sheen of surrounding marble. From what Kira could see around her, they were a little off course geographically, having stepped out of the doorway halfway up the Capitoline Hill; but as for temporally - time was truly out of joint. When they had first visited Ancient Rome, it had been in broad daylight and Kira, Chloe and their now lost brother Max had waited until evening to try to retrieve the dagger. On their return visit - it was already night and a spectacularly stormy one at that.

The wind whistled through the empty streets and alleyways, rattling shutters to accompany the sound of grumbling thunder.

"Are you not moved, when all the sway of earth shakes like a thing unfirm?" proclaimed Shakespeare.

"Are you quoting yourself again?" asked Kira in amazement at how self-obsessed Shakespeare had become after learning of his historical fame. The journey from one time to another ironically took no time at all but he had managed to find five or six quotes for the occasion - and all his own.

"Aye, but look - this is the tempest that did predict the death of Caesar. It is the very night before he was murdered!" Shakespeare was wide-eyed and fascinated again.

"If you say so," dismissed Kira as more thunder broke and rolled in the heavens.

Lucius was scared - to him this storm was an omen; a punishment from the gods for the mistakes of man. He understood what Shakespeare meant. "We should move from the streets," he said, "It isn't safe to be out in this."

"Someone doesn't think so," Chloe pointed out, and sure enough flitting from shadow to shadow, occasionally illuminated by the bursts of the 'heavens' fire', was a hooded figure. Kira looked. No, there were two people - both heavily cloaked in the swathes of their dark capes on this most eerie of nights. The lead figure strode purposefully ahead; taller and leaner he clearly had somewhere he needed to be. The other followed in short bursts of speed, moving rather like a startled partridge on a country road - he was much shorter and rounder and clearly less keen.

"They are the faction!" whispered Shakespeare, "O, conspiracy!"

Kira was just about to tell England's greatest dramatist to button it when she realised he may actually have a point. The shorter, rounder and clearly less athletic of the two could easily have been Casca - the gossip and food-loving Roman they had overheard in the Market Place yesterday: or earlier today; or - recently. Kira made a mental note to delete as appropriate when she had a few more facts about their current time and date. "Lucius?" she asked, "Which way to your master's house?"

Lucius indicated that the villa lay beyond the Capitoline Hill - in the very direction that the two shrouded figures were heading.

"Do you think Max will be at Brutus' house?" asked Chloe.

"Not really, but those two seem to be going to Brutus' house and we may find something out. After all, the conspiracy can't succeed without the murder weapon," Kira tapped her side where the dagger was tucked into her belt. At this stage, she didn't even want to think about the fact that when they lost Max, he had the dagger too. Who knew if two versions of the same thing, from two different times, could exist in one place together? Perhaps, she thought fleetingly, she could write a manual for time-travellers - after all, the only current reference works were science-fiction and most of them gave the impression that meeting a past or future version of yourself was a very bad idea. How would that work for objects though?

"Brutus?" Now Shakespeare was excited again, "Brutus? Marcus Junius Brutus?"

"He is my master, yes," Lucius answered.

Shakespeare had gone into meltdown over the thought of meeting the real protagonist of his latest play. "Imagine!" he gushed, "Imagine if I were to speak to Brutus. What character insights I should gain. What improvements I could make to my play."

"No," said Kira putting a stop to that nonsense. The thought of a 16th Century dramatist interviewing a Roman from before the 1st Millennia to find out his *motivation* was as far removed from her worries as it was possible to be right now. "However, Brutus' villa is as good a place to start as any," she turned to Lucius, "Are you sure you want to return to Brutus' service? You don't have to. Go back to slavery, I mean."

"It is all I know," Lucius said, sadly, "Brutus and Portia are my family."

It was truly sad - here was a young boy whose only vision for his life was a return to slavery. Kira and Chloe were deeply moved. Shakespeare, on the other hand, clearly did not care, "Most excellent!" he cried and Kira did something that she really wished she would be able to tell someone about - she kicked Shakespeare; really hard on the shin.

"Zounds!" he yelled.

"Nothing less than you deserve," she berated him, "One of the things we were told about you in class was that you had a clear understanding of the human condition. I disagree, you are selfish and all you think about are your plays."

"'Tis my job," he reasoned, rubbing his left leg.

"And it is my job to get my brother back and see that Lucius is safe; and then - take you back where you belong!" she suddenly remembered the first folio of his complete works that he had taken from the library. Here was a way of punishing him for his insensitivity, "And while we are about it, Shakespeare, hand it over."

"I know not what you mean," Shakespeare stammered, as much taken aback by this outspoken girl as by the request.

"The book shaped lump in your doublet gives it away," Kira pointed out.

"But, 'tis my future," Shakespeare begged.

"And that is where it must stay. I have to repair the damage we may have done and put everything back in its place and I am starting right now - hand it over," Kira demanded.

Unbuttoning his doublet, Shakespeare removed the tattered copy of his collected works and held it out for Kira with his head turned away from her. It was just as well that he wasn't looking as she took the unbelievably valuable book, strode a few metres down the hill to a nearby fountain and irreverently dropped it in. Hearing the splash, Shakespeare turned back to see Kira marching towards him, the fountain pool a little choppier than usual.

"My works," he gasped.

"Will come to you in time," she said, putting an end to any further discussion and confident that the waters of a Roman fountain would erase Shakespeare's words from this particular period of history. Kira turned to Lucius and smiled, thinking that his adventure was almost at an end. "Would you lead us to your master's house, please?" she asked. Lucius smiled and nodded, he was glad to be in familiar surroundings and would be pleased to lead his friends out of this unnatural storm.

It had started to rain as they made their way up the Capitoline Hill towards the Forum. The water ran down the smooth marble frontages of the various temples and official buildings and gave them extra gloss to reflect the sharp electric flashes in the sky. Ahead, they could just make out the hurrying shapes of the two hooded figures who did indeed appear to be heading for the very same villa. Shakespeare was sulking. He had lost interest in his surroundings, ceased quoting himself and was walking with his arms folded across his chest. Kira, Chloe and Lucius exchanged smiles as they tried, and failed, to get his attention. Guided by Lucius, they took an alleyway to the right at the far end of the empty Forum and, the two hooded figures were no longer there. They had vanished after definitely turning up this way. With no time to solve a further mystery, the children and Shakespeare continued up the alley.

Just over half way, a lamp lit window and low voices attracted their attention. Too high to get a good view, even for the relatively tall Shakespeare, Kira beckoned for Lucius to stop and they listened for a moment. A lightning flash illuminated the front of the dwelling - a creamy coloured stone house with stairs leading up into an alcove that must have been the main doorway. A heavy curtain was drawn at the top of the stairs and from the window, long moving shadows spilled into the street below. There were three shadows and the hushed voices were from three men.

"He is held highly and commands great respect," said one.

"If we could only get him to understand our cause, Cassius," said another.

"Cinna, my friend, before this night is out he will join us, mark my words," came the familiar and direct tone of Caius Cassius, ringleader of the conspirators.

"I was right!" said Shakespeare from below - in a loud stage-whisper and snapping instantly from his self-pity.

"And so modest," returned Kira. However, it seemed that Shakespeare could well have been right - the evidence was mounting for convincing proof that this was indeed the night before *The Ides of March*. If this were the case, the dagger had brought them back much later than their original visit and Sir Walter was very wrong about the fixed points at the start and end of these journeys through time. From the conversation in the house, it also seemed likely that the time-travelling quorum had followed two of the conspirators, Cassius and Casca, as they gathered fellow assassins for their cause. Reluctantly, Kira turned to Shakespeare for advice. "Shakespeare, where did you get your source material from for your play?" she quizzed.

"For *Julius Caesar*? Why from Plutarch. From his *Lives of the Noble Grecians and Romans*. 'Twas newly translated," Shakespeare informed her with a confused look, unsure of why she needed this information.

"And Plutarch was a historian?" she continued.

"Aye, from Ancient Greece," Shakespeare answered.

"So providing he was accurate, we can work out roughly what happens next. I definitely don't think we should get caught up in a massive historical incident like Caesar's assassination," warned Kira.

"I fail to see the method in thy madness," Shakespeare growled, clearly angry at not being allowed to get first hand experience of the main event of his play.

"Shakespeare, listen," Kira spoke directly to him, "Your play needs nothing else. I can assure you that it is remembered and well liked by many for years to come. If we influence any of the events that are building around us, even in the smallest of ways, we risk changing the History of the World. Who knows what would happen if Caesar survived his assassination just because you tried to direct the proceedings to make the assassination more dramatic. You can do that when we get back to 1599 - you can add, move, re-write, re-structure and change any part of your play. But this is real and there *are* consequences. Imagine for one moment that a distant Italian ancestor of the Shakespeare family is killed by Julius Caesar in 42 B.C. - all because Caesar was able to because he wasn't assassinated on The Ides of March in 44 B.C. No distant ancestor of the Shakespeares means no William

Shakespeare - and that means no plays."

Shakespeare was silent. Kira would like to have thought that it was because he was now aware of the consequences of changing such a major event, but she thought it more likely it was because she had told him there would be no plays. Whatever the reason, he stood down and bowed, literally, to her argument.

"Decius and Trebonius are already on their way," said Cassius from inside.

"Then we only need Metellus Cimber," said Casca.

"We could meet him at his house," said the other, named as Cinna by Cassius earlier.

In the alley outside, the tension of what to do next was mounting. "They are coming out," said a panicked Chloe - and they were. The flickering oil lamp was being carried away from the window as the three assassins prepared to leave.

"Lucius," said Kira with real urgency, "Do you know where Metellus Cimber lives?"

"I do, Kira, he has a small house a quarter of a league from here," answered Lucius.

"Which way, Lucius?" Kira was frantic now. The lamp light had gone from the window and could be seen through the gaps of the curtain in the alcove, heading towards the door. A flash of lightning illuminated the tense conversation for a split-second and Lucius pointed down the alleyway - the way they had come.

"I hope you're right," Kira smiled, having every faith in the little Roman, "Run!"

It made for a truly comic sight: a teenage girl in Elizabethan men's' clothing with a fake beard swinging around her throat like a hairy necklace; followed by an Elizabethan page boy, a Roman slave-boy and the infamous Elizabethan dramatist William

Shakespeare - all careering up an alleyway in Rome on the stormy night, very probably, preceding The Ides of March in 44 B.C.

Rounding a bend, they skidded to a halt and breathlessly listened for signs of anyone coming this way. There were none.

"What now?" asked Chloe.

"Precisely," panted Kira after her sprint, "What happens now, Shakespeare?"

"'Twas widely reported that the conspirators did meet at Brutus' house to prepare for what must be done in the morning," Shakespeare recounted.

"Then we carry on there," said Kira, "And whatever happens, we avoid any contact of any kind with any conspirators. Right, Shakespeare?"

Shakespeare cast a squinted look of disappointment and, as he moved to follow the three youngsters, muttered, "So wise so young, they say do never live long."

Chapter Nineteen

The rain had stopped, the thunder and lightning were distant echoes and the two Foster sisters were standing at that low, white-washed wall again - this time with two historical figures: Lucius Martius, little known slave-boy of Brutus; and William Shakespeare, well known dramatist of the Elizabethan Age. The rear gates to Brutus' orchard were tantalisingly close and Lucius couldn't help but watch them; hoping perhaps that his master would emerge and welcome him back to his familiar life of servitude.

"'Tis really Brutus' orchard beyond yonder gates?" Shakespeare asked.

"It is," answered Kira with a warning scowl - just to remind him of their newly created policy of non-intervention. Kira spoke urgently to Lucius, "We need some information, Lucius. We need to find out what has happened to Max."

"He will be OK - won't he, Kira?" Chloe urged.

"Of course," said Kira, deliberately ignoring the dangerous and volatile aspects of Ancient History, "He's probably loving *Hands on* History." Kira put her arm on Lucius shoulder, "What will you say to Brutus?" she asked.

"Just that I was lost but have come back of my own free will to return to my duties," he said.

"What if he gets cross?" said Chloe with genuine care and worry.

"Brutus is a good man. He doesn't beat me," Lucius said and Kira marvelled at this humble approach. Lucius had clearly accepted *his lot* in life and looked forward to nothing more than knowing he wouldn't be beaten. "I will find out what happened to Maximus," he added and started to walk to the gates.

"Wait!" cried Chloe, "Don't go. Come back with us. Our parents are rubbish they would never notice."

Chloe had a point and Kira could picture her Dad removing his ridiculous new spectacles, scratching his head and saying, "Four? But, I thought we only had three children?"

"No, Chloe," Lucius was honoured but bound by loyalty to decline, "Thank you, but no. I have seen the most amazing things today. Things that I fear I will never understand. This is my home and Brutus is my master and here is the only family I have."

Chloe ran the few steps to Lucius and, flinging her arms around him, stretched to give him a big kiss. Kira and Shakespeare exchanged smiles at the innocence of the situation then both joined Chloe at Lucius' side.

"Fare thee well, young Lucius," said William Shakespeare.

"Goodbye, Lucius. You really are the nicest Ancient Roman I have ever met," said Kira, ruffling his hair - because at fourteen, one simply didn't hug much younger boys. With that, Lucius Martius, genuine Roman slave, turned and walked to the orchard gates. Kira rubbed her right eye behind her glasses' lens to quickly conceal a tear.

However, Lucius was going nowhere. The gates appeared to be locked and would not budge - and, something else very strange was happening. The dagger in Kira's belt was buzzing faintly and getting strangely warm. Kira lifted her doublet and saw the blade vibrating faintly.

Aware that something was not quite right, Chloe asked, "What's the matter?"

"It's the dagger. It sounds silly, I know, but it's getting warm," Kira put her hand to the pommel and was alarmed to get a sharp electric shock.

"The gates are stuck," called Lucius from the archway.

"Maybe Brutus locked them," reasoned Kira as she rubbed her jolted hand, dismissing it as a freak side-effect from the night's storm.

"There is no lock on these gates," said Lucius and he started to knock hard for attention from within.

Brutus couldn't sleep. His mind was too full and the storm had made him uneasy. Portia had spent a while praying to the household gods but the combined charged atmosphere - of worries and storm static - had refused to go away. He knew he would get a visit tonight. He had had letters thrown in at his window over the last few weeks, telling him to wake up and save Rome. Though these messages were coded, he knew they had one meaning and, as he stood under the shelter of the porch looking out into the dark orchard, he contemplated the action needed to stop Julius Caesar.

It had to be by his death -

There was a hammering at the gate at the far end of the orchard. Brutus snapped out of his monstrous thoughts and muttered, "They are here." Stepping from under the pan-tiled roof, he knew he had little choice if he wanted to preserve the democracy of Rome. "Boy!" he called back into the house but there was no answer. "Boy!" he tried again and, eventually, a tired, scruffy looking lad of very nearly twelve years of age shuffled through the back door of the villa. His hair was messy - it had grown longer than he normally wore it and his face was dirty. He had been absolutely fast asleep.

"You called, Lord Brutus," he mumbled, wiping the sleep from his eyes with clenched fists.

"You sleep soundly, boy," Brutus smiled down at him.

"It's quite tough, you know - slavery," the boy responded in a rather insubordinate manner.

"There's somebody knocking at the gate," Brutus informed him.

The slave-boy looked up at Brutus, wondering if he knew

about the harmful effects of sleep-deprivation, "I'll go then shall I? I'll go and let in the murderers - who are the only ones dangerous enough to be out at this time of night." He mimed opening the gate and greeting them, "Good evening. Would you like to stab me now or shall I get you a drink first?"

"If you had not lost Lucius, you would be free," Brutus retorted.

"It gets abolished you know, slavery. It takes quite a long time but it does get abolished. Just - hold that thought, Master. Besides, I didn't lose Lucius - I lost my family," said the boy rebelliously and with an impossible knowledge of times to come.

"The gate, *Maximus*!" ordered his master.

The gates would not budge. No matter how Lucius tugged and pushed to get in, they were held fast. Chloe ran to help but was too small to make much of a difference. Seeing it as a chance to get into Brutus' garden whilst appearing to help the common cause, Shakespeare bounded over, "Forsooth, minions," he proclaimed, "Stand back and I will show thee how 'tis done." Taking a while to limber up with what must have been some weird actor-type warm-up; he rushed at the gates shoulder-first, and promptly ricocheted back off them flying several metres through the air and cursing as he stumbled past the children.

Even in the direst of situations, there was always time for a laugh and Kira could not resist a pun. "The gates must be Bard!" she chuckled; but no one with her understood the play on words. She started to stroll towards the gates to assist - but, it was like walking through very deep treacle. Every step she took got heavier and harder and to add to it, the dagger was vibrating furiously and getting very hot indeed. "Something's gone wrong," she yelled as a twisting wind sprang up from around her feet and blew tornado-like about them, churning up leaves, twigs and splats of mud.

The dagger was now vibrating at such a speed that it actually began to hurt. Crackles of blue electricity flew noisily back and forth around Kira and the rest of the group. The dagger was burning at her side. Pulling her fake beard necklace from around her neck, Kira used it to grab at the smouldering handle of the hot and highly animated dagger and yanked it from her belt. Then, as if repelled by an impossibly strong magnet, it flew out of her grip and back into the street away from the gates, clattering across the flagstones.

Incredibly, the wind dropped immediately, the noise disappeared instantly and the gates opened straight away.

There was no time to think about how this fitted in with the known laws of physics, as in front of them, in the archway of Brutus' orchard and framed by the white outside wall, stood a small and very uncombed young lad.

"Max!" cried Kira and Chloe together - and they ran as fast as they could. On hindsight, it was more of a rugby tackle than a hug but the intention was a good one. The three Foster siblings were violently and joyously re-united - in an untidy heap at the bottom of Brutus' garden in Ancient Rome. There was lots of giggling and when the three separated, Max had the first word - as usual.

"This *really* is Ancient Rome," he explained, as if this information were new to anyone.

"We know," laughed Kira - actually pleased to see her usually annoying brother.

"Lucius!" called Max, in greeting, to the Roman boy who smiled politely back. "And he," said Max aghast, "Looks like Shakespeare!"

"Heavens, my fame hath reached Ancient Rome," Shakespeare dreamed.

"It is Shakespeare," said Chloe, "We got him in 1599." Chloe spoke as if he were part of a historical sticker collection. If that were so, Kira would gladly have swapped him for someone less long-winded.

"In? What? Where have you been?" Max was struggling with a few concepts here.

"We are taking him back, as soon as we figure out how we need to leave things here," answered Kira.

"Taking him back to 1599? Can I come?" asked Max, excitedly, "Please?"

Kira stood and pulled Chloe to her feet. "I'll think about it," she teased.

Max picked himself up and the questions flooded randomly in, "How did you get to 1599? More to the point, why did you go to 1599? Even more to the point, what are you two wearing?" Max was referring to their Elizabethan *disguises*.

"You can talk," retorted Kira as she looked his genuine, brown, Roman-slave-style tunic up and down.

"This is my day job," Max scowled, "Twenty-four hours a day job. I have a job now. Eleven years old and, I have a job. I take it you can see I've been here a while." Max's hair was much longer and he needed a good wash and brush up. "I've been here a month. What kept you?"

"Whatever do you mean?" said Kira, knowing exactly what he meant.

"You know what I mean," Max spluttered, "I've fetched water from the well at all hours, cleaned the hypocaust grates daily, scrubbed the tiny tiles in mosaics, fetched oil lamps at the most unhealthy hours, prepared horrid food - sparrows, larks, otters, you name it and they eat it!" He turned to Lucius, "If you want your old job back, it is yours. I've had it with slavery."

Kira started to laugh - not really because Max had had to do all that work, although that was quite funny, but because she had forgotten how entertaining her little brother could be. "This time thing is incredible. We're still on the same day in 2021," she smiled.

Max huffed his over-long fringe from his eyes and moaned,

"Incredible? Incredibly unfair, yeah!"

"Maximus?" There was a shout from near to the house.

"Brutus," groaned Max.

"Brutus!" exclaimed Shakespeare.

"Master Brutus," smiled Lucius.

Kira looked thoughtfully in the direction of the call and pushed her glasses back to the bridge of her nose. She was thinking again. "How did you end up working for Brutus?" she asked.

"Simple Roman justice," said Max, "The very simple Roman soldier who grabbed me - you remember Crassus, don't you? - had the great idea that as Brutus had lost a slave, he needed a replacement." His voice dropped an octave, "I am the replacement."

Kira's thinking was leading her to the vital question. "What happened to the dagger, Max?" she asked, sincerely.

"That's here too," Max replied, cheerfully, "Brutus has it. Crassus said he didn't need two blades to 'uphold Roman Law' - or something."

"Right," said Kira with a distant expression on her face, "Only we've got the dagger too," she paused and pointed down the alley, "There."

The dagger was there. It now lay motionless and quiet after, quite literally, kicking up a storm.

"Maximus!" came Brutus' call again.

"What shall I do?" asked Max.

"One moment," Kira said, mysteriously - and she strode purposefully back down the alley to the dagger that killed Julius Caesar. She paused and stared down at it. "Two daggers," she said, as if talking to the one in front of her. She looked back up the alley to where Lucius, Shakespeare and her brother and sister stood. "Two daggers in the same place," she mused, "Not just two daggers but the same dagger - twice."

"I wonder if time-travel rots the mind?" asked a bemused Max.

Then, it started again - Kira picked the dagger from the floor and it began to hum lightly. She took a few steps back towards Brutus' villa and it began to vibrate. She took a few more steps and it started to heat up in her hand. A few more and it was shaking wildly and almost too hot to touch. More still and a sudden wind blew up and whirled around the group with real intensity. Blue sparks leapt back and forth from the orchard gates to Kira and then - the dagger was forced back out of her hand to clatter into the alley once more.

"Would you mind letting us mere mortals in on any theories you may be working on?" said Max at his most sarcastic, "And don't you dare say, 'I'll tell you later'!"

Kira simply said, "We can go."

"Go?" asked Chloe.

"Home," said Kira.

"Maximus!" came an irate shout from Brutus' yard.

"Allow me," said Lucius stepping to the gate.

"Would you, really?" asked Max, incredulously.

"It is my place and time," Lucius said - and before there could be further farewells, hugs or 'thank yous', he had run through the gateway and into the darkness of the familiar orchard.

There was a wooden plaque on the wall in the kitchen at home that read - 'Enjoy the little things in life, for someday you will realise they were the big things'. Parting company with this brave and cheerful Roman orphan - who saw himself as a very small cog in the infinite universal machine - was one such small thing that meant so much. Lucius was an incredible example of selflessness and as they listened to the echoed cries of his name shouted in joy and disbelief in the distance by Portia and Brutus, they knew that Lucius was appreciated in some small way. Freeing Max from slavery, which in the grand scheme of the assassination plot growing around them - was very minor, had allowed all three of the Foster children to leave. They all had a lot to be very grateful to Lucius Martius for.

"He was the noblest Roman of them all," said Shakespeare - self-quoting again but in profound tribute for once.

The tribute, however, was to be short-lived as there were many figures coming up the alleyway in the distance - seven of them; all cloaked and hooded.

"They are the conspirators!" whispered Shakespeare - conspiratorially counting cloaks, "My, 'tis just like my play!"

"Surely, your play is just like *this*," suggested Kira.

"Art thou suggesting plagiarism?"

"No, I am suggesting concealment. Behind the wall," urged Kira, "We have to keep out of this."

"The dagger," shrieked Chloe, "They are going to walk right over it."

"Leave matters to me," said Shakespeare with genuine bravado, "Conceal yourselves and I will retrieve the dagger."

Though Kira had the distinct and unnerving feeling that letting Shakespeare take control was a very bad move, she had no time for any other option and nodded her agreement.

"Quick," said Max - who was helping Chloe over the low wall to join him. Kira scrambled behind to join them and watched in hidden amazement. Shakespeare - who in doublet, hose and tights blended into his surroundings like the infamous elephant in the room of linguistic legend - strode nonchalantly towards the seven, robed men whom he must have known were armed.

"Who's there?" demanded one of the sinister hoodies as they got closer to him.

"A Roman," answered Shakespeare, unconvincingly, "What

night is this?" Shakespeare was gesturing grandly to the heavens.

"Oh, I don't believe it," whispered Kira behind the wall.

"What?" asked Max.

"He is using one of his own scenes to distract the conspirators. Is there no end to the vanity of this man?" Kira went on.

"It's working though, look," pointed Chloe.

Indeed, Shakespeare was standing on the dagger to keep it from the attentions of the conspirators.

"A very pleasing night for honest men," said the lead conspirator.

"Who ever knew the heavens menace so?" quoted Shakespeare in conversation - but it was in vain for he received no answer from his shrouded audience and added quickly, "Good night, gentlemen. This disturbed sky is not to walk in." He paused and then, most unconvincing of all stooped to draw attention to the dagger. You could almost hear the disbelief from behind the wall as he said, "Is this a dagger which I see before me?" and grasping it, "Come, let me clutch thee!" Then, he strode off down the alleyway in blissful, oblivious performance manner.

The conspiratorial group paused and looked at each other - and then, they laughed.

"Another crazy soothsayer," said one amidst the derisive laughs.

Max was of a mind to leap out in defence of soothsayers but thought it probably best not to lose his life over a reckless outburst for misplaced injustice. The cloaked group had re-doubled their purpose and were now approaching the gates of the orchard. Mere metres away, the Foster siblings crouched, willing the darkness to keep them concealed. One of the men was now banging on the wooden gates. A few further knocks and a chink of lamplight appeared, followed by the familiar face of Lucius. It was to be the last time they saw their Roman friend as he stepped back into the darkness to let in the conspiracy then closed the gates on his friends from the future.

"Quickly," said Kira, jumping up, "We need to see Shakespeare."

Not a phrase you would ever expect a fourteen-year-old girl to say.

He hadn't gotten far. Looking very pleased with his efforts, he was sitting on some temple steps where the alley re-joined the Forum, waiting. Kira, Chloe and Max tore round the corner and slid to a halt at his feet.

"The dagger, child," he said offering the handle to Kira.

"Thank you, sir," Kira curtseyed badly, "We can go now."

"I meant to ask you about that," said Max, "The special effects when you picked up the dagger - you said it meant we can go home. Please explain."

"It was something I was thinking about when we arrived back here," Kira said, waving the dagger, "We had to fetch the dagger from Shakespeare's time because I knew that the only way we could rescue you was with the dagger."

Max could only manage, "Eh?"

"You got stuck here with the only means of rescuing you in your hand."

"Right," Max said slowly.

"So the only way we could get back to you was to get the dagger back - because the dagger was what enabled us to get here in the first place. And if it was with you and we couldn't get to you, we needed to get it from somewhere else."

"Am with you," Max lied.

"Sir Walter told us that all of the objects enabled anyone leaving the Cabinet of Curiosities carrying them to travel to the point in time where the object was used and we knew that the dagger had had a long history. We knew that it had ended up in the possession of an actor in Shakespeare's theatre so we used the quill from the Cabinet of Curiosities to go back to 1599 and grab the dagger later on in its history."

"So we could take it to the Cabinet and then come back to Rome," added Chloe, perceptively for her six years.

"We picked up a stowaway along the way. He followed us back to Kensington Castle," Kira indicated Shakespeare who bowed facetiously, "And when we arrived back in Rome, I knew something was wrong as we were much later in time and half a mile or so from the Market Place - even though Sir Walter assured us that we would always travel to fixed points and exact times."

"But the special effects?" Max urged.

"I'm getting to that," she snapped, "The closer I took the dagger to Brutus' house the more strangely it behaved - glowing, vibrating, getting hot, causing storms and so on. When we found you, you gave us the answer."

"I did?" Max was unsure.

"You did," Kira was sure, "You said that the dagger that you got stuck here with was given to Brutus. That wasn't just *a* dagger, it was *this* dagger."

"I get it!" Max yelled a good guess, "A future or past version of an object can't exist in the same time with another version of the same object."

"Well, I'm no expert but it would explain us being off course, being much later and having the *special effects* as you call them." Kira had her first chapter for her future book of time-travel - probable proof that two versions of the same object could not occupy the same time and space - maybe. "Anyway," she continued, "We now know that it is Brutus and not Cassius that uses the dagger to assassinate Caesar as he has a version of it in his house."

"That Crassus gave him," interjected Max.

"So all our accidental interference is put right and everything is back where it should be," Kira finished.

And then, she looked at William Shakespeare.

Chapter Twenty

There was a definite need for a historical Satnav - thought Max, a little later on. Set Country - England; set place - London; set Time - 1599; set Via Point - 2021; Acquiring time lines; Calculating years - two thousand, four hundred and eighty-seven years in total; time to destination - instant.

The brief stop in Kensington Castle was merely to collect the quill but several unsuccessful attempts to get Shakespeare back to his own time had followed. After the fifth return to the Market Place in Rome, it was Kira that realised that only the object used to travel should be held and any other items from the collection which may need transporting had to be hidden - maybe they caused *temporal interference*, or something. Stuffing the dagger down Shakespeare's doublet was the solution of how to take it back to 1599 and with Chloe holding the quill in her hand, the four travellers finally connected 2021 to the end of the 16th Century.

The oak door opened into the yard of *The Globe Theatre* and Max took his first breath of Elizabethan air.

"Rancid!" he exclaimed, "Ancient Rome smelled better."

"Ah," said Shakespeare, "That will be the fact that this very theatre is built upon a marsh."

"Not to mention that everyone throws all their waste into the street to rot," added Kira.

Upon the stage, Burbage was pacing back and forth in front of the small round boy auditioning for the part of Lucius. He had lost something. Spotting Shakespeare in the shadows of the yard, he boomed, "Will, hast thou seen my sword?"

Shakespeare reached into his doublet and stabbed his hand, "Aye!" he yelled in pain, "I did find it earlier." He waved the dagger to a relieved Burbage. It was now back where it should be.

"Earlier in 44 B.C." chuckled Kira.

Burbage strode from the stage to collect his precious sword and caught sight of Kira and Chloe, still in male Elizabethan dress. "More lads for the role of Lucius, Will?" he roared - demonstrating no recollection of them and showing he had clearly never met them before and thus - proving they had returned to exactly the same hour as before.

"Not exactly," answered Kira quickly, before Shakespeare could somehow rope them in disastrously in.

"But who is this poor urchin?" asked Burbage looking at the dishevelled state of Max.

"Verily, Burbage," started Shakespeare, "This lad hath first hand experience of the character. He hath *lived* slavery!"

"Aye?" asked Burbage.

"Aye," confirmed Shakespeare.

Kira could see where this was going and shifted the attention to the stage, asking, "And who is this lad? He looks the part to me."

The boy on the stage shifted uncomfortably. He was stout and round and about as far removed from the real Lucius as could be.

"This is Master William Rowley," announced Burbage, "Methinks, he won't amount to much - except a good size." Burbage chuckled at the expense of Rowley.

"Nevertheless," continued Kira, "We should definitely hear him."

"Verily?" asked Shakespeare.

"Aye," said Kira in period unsteadiness, "- Verily."

"Very good Master Rowley, we will hear thy performance," agreed Shakespeare.

"Thank you kindly, Mister Slackplayer," said Rowley.

Shakespeare said nothing. No shouting, no correction, no

dismissal. Burbage stared at him. "Art thou well, Will?" he asked.

"Aye, Richard," Shakespeare replied.

"But, thy name, Will?" Burbage pointed out.

"Will be remembered, Burbage," Shakespeare said with a smile, "In time."

It was a prophetic moment to leave the 16th Century and return to tidy up a few loose ends. Kira and Chloe needed to change back to their own non-historic clothing and Max? Well the best Max could hope for was that there was a comb in The Cabinet of Curiosities. As for what had happened to his clothes, there would have to be a seriously creative story agreed by all to explain that one away.

"And this is Sir Walter's thirteenth bathroom. The very last on our tour," droned the Tour Guide as the oak door opened and two girls and a Roman slave entered quietly. There was a general sigh of relief from the tortured visitors. "The very last bathroom that is - plenty of other rooms though!" she enthused over the muffled groans of what seemed to have become the inmates of Kensington Prison - doing life sentences. "Notice the continued themes throughout the house before we proceed to the second, minor, lesser Hall-Annexe - where we will be having something very special!" she paused for an imaginary drum roll, "A quiz! With questions on everything you have learnt today." Max could have sworn he heard the sound of several expiring bodies hitting the polished oak floor. There was certainly a perceptibly louder groan. "That's the spirit - come along!" and the Tour Guide marched through another door to her fun Kensington Castle - EXAM.

The children stayed put. Watching their parents drift through like over-educated zombies.

"Eventful day," said Kira.

"Yeah. Delivered a prophecy, supplied a murder weapon,

broke into a Roman house, profaned a temple, got arrested, was sold into slavery, got rescued by three Elizabethans and then dropped Shakespeare home. It seemed to last a month. I'm quite tired now!" said Max.

"Me too," yawned Chloe - who had also been awake for nearly forty-eight hours in one day.

"Bet Mum and Dad are asleep, listening to that guide. I mean, there is only so much about oak that it is healthy to know!" laughed Kira.

The door that had just closed, after the tour group went through, opened again. It was Mrs. Foster and she looked cross.

"Maximillian William Foster," she called and, with full name usage, he knew he was in trouble, "What on earth do you look like? What are you wearing?"

"Historical re-enactment," blurted Kira, very quickly.

"Historical re-enactment?" queried Mum.

"Ah, yes," Kira continued to dig a big hole for Max, "Romans - versus Tudors."

"And Tudors won by the looks of things!" she said, turning back to call into the other room, "Michael? Michael! Just look at the state of your son. He's gone all - Roman. And when was the last time he had a hair cut - you will really have to take him. He can't go to school looking like that." Her protestations got quieter as she re-entered the tour and moved off with the rest of the group.

The Foster children were alone again. Kira giggled but Max was far from amused. There was little chance of retrieving his clothing and he was very worried that this would be the excuse Mum needed to get him into those three-quarter length woollen shorts. Kira's phone bleeped an awful lot as she turned it back on after the supernatural crisis of the Elizabethan low battery alert. It caught up with the twenty-first century and she quickly soaked up the information on the screen. Things were returning to normal.

Chloe had sat on an ottoman that she probably shouldn't have but who was going to tell a time-travelling six-year-old what to do. She fought hard to stay awake and listen.

"Thirty-six messages, twenty-two missed calls and fifty-seven people have written on my wall," Kira announced proudly, "But, five percent battery, no!"

"Must be those *selfies* you took outside the temple," Max joked and Kira smiled. "You didn't?" he asked.

"I went on holiday to Rome, that's all," she grinned.

"There is one thing I can't work out," said Max, "You said that the items in The Cabinet of Curiosities take you to where they were used."

"Ahuh," said Kira, texting.

"How come we went to that point in Ancient Rome then?" he puzzled.

"How do you mean?" Kira was concentrating again.

"Well, the dagger first took us to about a month before it was… it was 'used'," Max said, clearly referencing the assassination of Julius Caesar.

"I don't know," said Kira. That particular chapter in her future book of time-travel obviously needed work.

"Do you think it had something to do with us? Something to do with what I was meant to do? The 'Ides of March prophecy thing', maybe?" he went on.

"Like it was always meant to happen, you mean? You were always supposed to be the soothsayer? A boy from 2021 was destined to travel back in time to accidentally warn Julius Caesar of the date of his murder? Bit far fetched. Not sure I would buy it… if it hadn't actually happened, that is." She was smiling - this was a mystery for another day.

"I just don't understand, really," said Max, "But I would like to find out somehow. There are more of History's mysteries here."

"Not today though, eh?" Kira pleaded.

"No. Not today," Max agreed.

"We could ask, Sir Walter," said Kira.

"We could if we knew where he was," Max agreed.

"Or *when* he was," Kira grinned.

Chloe had fallen asleep on the ottoman leaning against the wall. Kira gently picked her up and draped her sleeping form over her shoulder as she had done when Chloe was really small. She walked with her sleeping burden to the door to follow the tour group. This oak panelled door would lead to a quiz on Kensington Castle - and nothing else. They would probably do very badly on the questions about oak - but ask them a question on Ancient Rome or Shakespearean theatre and there would be success and smiles all round.

Kira, Max and a sleeping Chloe left Sir Walter Cope's thirteenth bathroom shattered yet satisfied with the day's outcome.

From another door at the other end of the bathroom, a concealed door, the impossibly old Sir Walter Cope watched them leave. He did have many more secrets; some of them very dark indeed. He knew about the power that existed in Kensington Castle and how it was created and *tamed*. He knew why the dagger had taken the children to Ancient Rome at the point in time that it did. He knew the real secret of time and how all events were connected. He could see the bigger picture and the web of fate that connected some very important events indeed. He knew the overall power and its dark intentions and was determined to try and contain everything - as he had done over the last four hundred and twenty-two years.

What was more, he knew *who* was behind it all and that was what frightened him most.

It *was* the most boring place on Earth.

But Kira, Max and Chloe Foster would come again.

––––––––––––

Acknowledgements

Although writing a book is a 'mostly' solo journey, I am extremely grateful for the advice, support, encouragement and coffee from the following very important people:

Tony, Carol and Fergus Bennett

Carol Graham

Sarah Hill

Erin Pollock

Richard and Sarah Whittle

And, without question, my wonderful wife and children.

Available worldwide from
Amazon and all good bookstores

Michael Terence
Publishing

www.mtp.agency

www.facebook.com/mtp.agency

@mtp_agency

Ingram Content Group UK Ltd.
Milton Keynes UK
UKHW040719220623
423745UK00018B/45

9 781800 942769